SPELL'S BELLS

A SPELLBOUND PARANORMAL COZY MYSTERY, BOOK 3

ANNABEL CHASE

RED PALM PRESS LLC

Spell's Bells

A Spellbound Paranormal Cozy Mystery, Book 3

By Annabel Chase

Copyright © 2017 Red Palm Press LLC

This is a work of fiction. Names, characters, businesses, places, events and incidents are either the products of the author's imagination or used in a fictitious manner. Any resemblance to actual persons, living or dead, or actual events is purely coincidental.

Cover Design by Alchemy

❀ Created with Vellum

To Fabio – your glistening pecs are a daily inspiration.

CHAPTER 1

I STOOD on the wraparound front porch of my large Victorian house, sweeping away the dirt. I gave myself bonus points for moving the two Adirondack chairs instead of simply sweeping around them.

"What do you think you're doing?" Gareth asked.

"What does it look like?" I stopped sweeping and leaned against the broom. "Fiona doesn't come until tomorrow." Fiona was the owner of the fairy cleaning service, The Magic Touch.

Gareth tried to wrest the broom from my hand, but since he was a ghost, he only managed to glide through the wooden handle.

"This is your brand new broom for flying, not sweeping," he said. Although I'd managed to successfully complete the first phase of broom training and get my daytime license, I had no intention of using it.

I examined the bright blue broom in my hand. Although I wanted one in Tiffany blue to match my wand, Broomstix didn't offer brooms in that color.

"It does the job just fine," I said and continued sweeping.

"You know perfectly well I have no intention of flying on it." Ever. Despite the aid of an anti-anxiety potion, I had no desire to voluntarily ride a wooden stick hundreds of feet above the ground.

Gareth rolled his eyes. "I hope you never encounter a broomstick emergency."

"As far as I'm concerned, the only broomstick emergency will involve dust or cobwebs." I swept the remaining debris off the porch and into the garden below.

"Some witch you are," Gareth said.

I ignored his comment and retreated into the house. I needed to feed Gareth's cat, Magpie, before he chewed off his own leg. I wouldn't put it past him.

"What's the best way to welcome a banshee into one's home? Do I need an offering of some kind? Maybe pig's blood?" If that was the case, I'd have to send my owl to the store pronto.

"A simple 'do come in' will suffice," Gareth replied.

Town council member and resident banshee Maeve McCullen was due to arrive at any moment. I'd invited her to the house to discuss my ability to see the ghost of Gareth, my dead vampire roommate. It was apparently unusual in Spellbound for a witch to communicate with the dead. Since banshees have a strong connection to death, we thought Maeve would be a good person to confide in.

The sound of wind chimes drifted through the kitchen and I froze with Magpie's dish in my hand. The hairless cat meowed at me from his position on the counter. He wasn't about to let an agent of death come between him and his tuna. I set the dish on the floor and hurried to the door with Gareth hot on my heels.

"Do I look presentable?" he asked.

"You're dead," I reminded him. "You're basically transparent."

"No need to be harsh," he said.

I opened the door to greet Maeve.

"Gareth," she exclaimed and leaned forward to literally air kiss him. "Death really suits you, darling."

"That's what they said when I first became a vampire," he replied.

"Every bit as true today," she said, fluffing her strawberry blond ringlets.

"Please come in," I said. As we began to walk toward the living room, Magpie shot out of nowhere and launched himself at Maeve's leg. He curled around her ankle and purred ferociously.

"Oh, you lovely creature." Maeve bent down and lifted him.

"Be careful," I warned.

Maeve held the ghastly cat an inch from her face. I covered my eyes, fearful that he'd strike at any moment, using claws or those ridiculously sharp teeth of his.

"Oh, Magpie. Your tongue is like sandpaper," she said with a tinkling laugh.

I peeked through my fingers to see Magpie licking her nose. What the…? "He really likes you," I said.

Maeve looked at me. "You sound surprised."

"Other than Gareth, I didn't think he liked anyone."

"I told you," Gareth said smugly. "He's very particular."

Maeve placed the cat gently on the floor. "Be kind to your new owner, feline. She's the one who keeps you reeking in tuna."

Magpie rubbed against her ankle, then hissed at me for good measure before trotting away.

"Can I offer you a drink?" I asked. "I have lemon fizz or maybe something stronger like a pomegranate pounder?"

She smiled. "Sounds like you're getting into the swing of things here."

"Slowly," I said.

"Why don't we sit in the living room where it's more comfortable?" Gareth said. It was odd for him to be able to act as host since, typically, I was the only one who could see him.

"I love what you've done in here," Maeve said, spinning around to admire the newer paint and window dressings. "No offense, darling, but Emma's taste is much more my style."

"None taken," Gareth mumbled. Oh boy. Now he'd sulk for the next twenty minutes. Didn't Maeve know better?

I planted myself on the settee and Maeve sat in the wing-back chair adjacent to me.

"So you'd like to know more about this unique situation, is that right?" Maeve gestured to Gareth, who hovered by the oversized fireplace.

"Whatever you can tell me," I said. "None of the witches in the coven can see ghosts. Is that a trait of my coven?" Although we knew my coven was different, the details were scarce.

Maeve crossed her legs and rested her hands on her knee. "I wish I could help, but I'm afraid my knowledge of covens is rather limited. I think you might be better off speaking to an older witch, one with more worldly experience."

"Like Lady Weatherby?" Lady J.R. Weatherby was the head of the Spellbound coven and the only witch I'd met so far that I was genuinely afraid of.

Maeve swatted the air. "Oh no, darling. I mean an *older* witch. Like Agnes."

"Good thinking," Gareth said. "I'd forgotten about her."

"That's because she's been in the Spellbound Care Home for ages," Maeve said. "She's a former head of the coven and very sharp. I'm sure she can offer you more insight than I can."

4

"Thanks," I said. "That's helpful." I wondered why no one in the coven had mentioned Agnes as a possible resource before. The mystery surrounding my origin was well known in Spellbound.

"Word to the wise, though," Maeve said. "You don't want to show up empty-handed. Sneak in a little contraband like sweets and alcohol and she'll be much more agreeable."

I made a mental note of her suggestion. If Agnes was as intimidating as Lady Weatherby, I was all for making her agreeable by whatever means necessary.

"You, my good man, are another story," Maeve said, focusing on Gareth. "I'd be happy to take you under my wing. I imagine you have many questions."

Gareth's relief was palpable. "Yes, I do. So many. Is it possible for me to make physical contact? I mean, I know I won't ever be in the flesh again, but can I at least move objects? I'd love to be able to slam a door once in a while, just to make a point." He narrowed his eyes at me.

Maeve twirled a strawberry blonde curl around her finger. "I can make a few recommendations. There are books on the subject." She hesitated. "My primary recommendation, though, is to enlist the aid of one of the Grey sisters. Any one of the three would make an excellent tutor."

Gareth made a choking noise. "You expect me to spend time alone with a Grey sister?"

Maeve shrugged. "You're already dead. What's the harm?"

I looked from Maeve to Gareth. "What's a Grey sister?"

"Three sisters who live in the northeastern hills of Spellbound," Maeve explained. "They rarely come into town."

"They share one eye and one tooth between them," Gareth said, shuddering.

"They're often mistaken for witches," Maeve added, "but they're more akin to goddesses."

"Wrinkled, ugly goddesses," Gareth complained. "Why

couldn't I have Markos as a tutor?" Markos was the town minotaur and widely known for his impressive physical attributes.

"So you think one of these blind, toothless old women will agree to Yoda him?" I asked.

Maeve frowned. "What does Yoda mean?"

It was bizarre to live in a world where a Yoda reference required explanation. "Never mind."

"I'll speak to the Grey sisters on your behalf," Maeve said. "Do you have a preference?"

Gareth groaned. "The one least likely to eat Emma."

"Um, yes. That sounds reasonable to me."

Maeve stood to go. "I'll be in touch, darling. Don't do anything I wouldn't do."

Gareth attempted to slump against the fireplace and disappeared inside the wall. "No worries," his muffled voice said. "I can't even do anything you *would* do."

Maeve was barely out of the house when Darcy Minor rode up the driveway on her magical bicycle. Darcy was the eldest of the youngest generation of Minors—one of six harpies that lived next door.

"Good. You're home," she said, striding up the walkway. "I need to speak with you urgently."

Me? No one ever needed to speak with me urgently.

"How can I help you, Darcy?"

She stomped up the porch steps and adjusted her frilly blouse. In a pencil skirt with perfectly coiffed hair, she was the fanciest harpy in town.

"Have you spoken to the Winged Wonder recently?" she demanded.

I could only assume she meant Daniel. "Not for a few days. Why?"

She crossed her arms. "He must be stopped. The angel is out of control."

My pulse quickened. "What do you mean?" Daniel Starr was a fallen angel with a long history of womanizing. Some stories claimed that he was the real reason for the town curse. He'd scorned an enchantress who then cursed the entire town—a curse that prevented the supernatural residents from crossing the Spellbound border. Daniel was, in fact, the reason I was here in the first place. He'd accidentally flown me across the boundary line, neither one of us aware of the fact that I was a witch.

She threw up her hands. "Every time I turn around, he's trying to do *good*. It's becoming a real problem."

"You're angry because Daniel is trying to be a positive force in Spellbound?"

"It's more than that. You know how I'm in charge of school fundraisers?"

Well, I knew she was the self-appointed martyr of Spellbound. "Sure," I said.

"Daniel's trying to horn in on my turf," she huffed. "He seems to think that turning over a new leaf means getting underfoot. Big mistake." She lifted her shoe. "These heels will crush him."

They would indeed. They were at least three inches high and very spiky. I wasn't sure how she walked in them without keeling over. Must be magic.

"What's he doing?" I knew his general plan was to stop moping and make a difference in our small world. He wanted to redeem himself for past transgressions. I didn't know the specifics regarding his reprehensible behavior. The Daniel I'd gotten to know since my arrival was very different from the one everyone in Spellbound seemed to know.

"He's organizing the bake sale," she said, near hysterics. "Everyone knows *I'm* in charge of the bake sale."

Beside me, Gareth rolled his eyes. "Her need for control is so over the top."

"Says the vampire who criticizes the way I wear my socks," I said.

"Either pull them up to your knees or don't wear knee socks at all," he said in exasperation.

Darcy squinted at me. "Are you talking to me?"

"No, sorry." I returned my attention to her. "So why have you come to me with this? Talk to Daniel."

"It's my understanding that the two of you have formed some weird and wonderful friendship. I was hoping you could have a word with him. Find some other way to satisfy his philanthropic needs."

Weird and wonderful. That was one way to describe our relationship.

"I'll see what I can do."

Darcy's pinched expression relaxed slightly. "Thank you. I mean, some of the high school girls are ecstatic to have a hot angel hanging around, but most of us think it's creepy."

I saw her point. "Do you need any help with the bake sale? I'm starting a magical baking class at the academy this week. I might be able to contribute."

"And poison the whole high school?" Gareth scoffed. "Don't even consider it."

"I'm not going to poison anyone," I said.

Darcy's eyes widened. "I should hope not."

I heard Sedgwick shrieking before I actually saw him.

"Duck," I yelled at Darcy.

We both crouched down at the same time to avoid getting knocked over by an owl.

I didn't even realize you were out, I said. Sedgwick was my familiar and we communicated telepathically.

I went out for a snack to my favorite place in the forest, he explained. *You need to come quickly. Grab your broom.*

"Sedgwick," I said aloud. "You know how I feel about riding on a broom."

It's an emergency, he shouted. *Sophie's being arrested as we speak.*

"What?" Sophie was one of the remedial witches in my class and a good friend.

Just come, Sedgwick insisted.

"I'm sorry, Darcy. I promise I'll speak to Daniel, but I need to go."

"Do you need a ride on my bicycle?" Darcy asked.

"No, thanks," I said. "I'll take Sigmund." Sigmund was my beloved 1988 green Volvo that I thought was forever lost at the bottom of Swan Lake. Daniel recently surprised me by retrieving the car from the lake and having it reengineered to run on magical energy instead of gasoline. It was the single sweetest thing anyone had ever done for me.

"Hold down the fort," I told Gareth and rushed past Darcy to the car.

Follow my lead, Sedgwick said.

I drove Sigmund on the road until we reached the edge of the forest. I parked the car and continued to follow the spotted owl into the woods.

"I don't see anyone," I said, running along a well-worn path.

Suddenly, I stopped running.

"What on earth…?"

In front of me was a glass coffin on a raised platform. More importantly, it wasn't empty.

This is why Sophie was arrested, Sedgwick said.

I ignored the yellow caution tape around the coffin and went to look inside. A dwarf lay in the coffin, his eyes closed and a bouquet of flowers in his hands.

"Is he dead?" I asked.

No. It's the Endless Sleep spell.

9

"Is that like a coma?"

I don't know what a coma is.

I peered at the dwarf inside. Although I'd met a few dwarfs during my brief time in Spellbound, he wasn't one of them.

"How could anyone think Sophie is responsible for this? She's the sweetest, clumsiest witch in all of Spellbound."

You'll have to ask Sheriff Hugo. I only saw him leading her away.

Ugh. I didn't want to speak with Sheriff Hugo. I was on the centaur's short list of Most Annoying Residents. I managed to get under his hide early on and never left.

Hop in that rolling piece of metal you call transportation, Sedgwick said. *You need to get to the sheriff's office before he does anything stupid.*

If he'd already arrested Sophie, then it was too late.

CHAPTER 2

SHERIFF HUGO GLANCED up from the newspaper when I walked into his office and I caught the flash of annoyance. To be fair, he didn't try to disguise it.

"Sheriff Hugo," I greeted him.

"Miss Hart." His gaze flickered to the corridor that presumably led to the holding cells. "I assume you're here about Miss Gale."

"I am." I tempered my tone, not wanting to push the wrong button. "You can't possibly believe that Sophie is responsible for the Endless Sleep spell. You know she's a remedial witch."

He tossed down the paper he was reading. "And it's a complicated spell. Yes, Miss Hart. Despite your best efforts to make me look like one, I am not an idiot."

Unsurprisingly, he was mistaken. I never set out to make him look like an idiot. He managed to do that all by himself.

"What makes her your prime suspect?" I asked.

"She was found at the scene with a wand in her hand."

"And?" I prompted. There had to be more than that.

"And she was alone."

I struggled to bite my tongue. When it came to police procedure, Spellbound rules were far more relaxed than those in the American human world.

"Has she said anything?" I asked.

He shrugged. "Says she didn't do it."

I strangled a scream. "Can I see her?"

He narrowed his eyes. "Not if you intend to start trouble."

My hands flew to my hips before I could stop them. "I *intend* to comfort my friend, who is probably very upset and scared."

He grunted and motioned me forward. "Third cell on the right. Five minutes."

I hurried down the corridor until I reached Sophie. There were no bars like in human jails, only an invisible barrier between the corridor and the tiny room.

Sophie stood at the invisible barrier, waiting. She clutched a tissue in her fist, the only sign that she'd been crying. "I heard your voice. I so hoped I wasn't imagining it."

I pressed my palms against the barrier. "Tell me what happened."

"I was gathering berries for our magical baking class tomorrow," she explained. "Last term Ginger had shared a recipe for burstberry muffins and I wanted to recreate it." Ginger was one of the few redheaded members of the coven. Although she was young, she sometimes acted as a substitute for Professor Holmes or Lady Weatherby.

"And you stumbled upon the coffin?"

She sniffed and nodded. "At first, I didn't realize anyone was inside. I thought maybe a vampire was using it as outdoor living space." A vampire version of a cabin in the woods. "Then I realized how short the length was and I knew it couldn't be meant for a vampire."

"Why did you draw your wand?" I asked. Sheriff Hugo said he'd found her holding her wand.

"When I looked inside and saw the dwarf's face, I panicked. I pulled out my wand and jumped backward." Her chin lowered. "I managed to trip on a rock and fell on my butt. That's when the sheriff arrived."

"Do you even know the dwarf?" I asked.

"I know his name is Freddie. We've interacted on occasion, but no. I don't know him well."

"Did you tell the sheriff what you told me?"

"Of course." She wiped a stray tear from her cheek. "He didn't care. He said I was the only one on the scene and he had to bring me in."

"Did you see anyone else while you were out there?"

She shook her head. "No. My owl was with me, but that's it."

"Did the sheriff say how he knew about the coffin?" I asked.

"No." Sophie placed her palms against the invisible barrier, mirroring mine. "Emma, I'm scared."

"Don't worry," I said. "I won't let him keep you here." I wasn't sure how I could secure her release, but not knowing how to do something wasn't a deterrent for me. Sophie was my friend—my sweet, innocent friend. I had no intention of letting her fall victim to the sheriff's lazy work ethic.

"My parents are on their way," Sophie said. "I'm sure they'll give the sheriff an earful, too."

I kissed the barrier and took a step back. "Stay strong. Let me see what I can do."

There was a question nagging me. On my way out of the office, I decided to get it off my chest.

"Sheriff?"

"No, I'm not going to release her, even if you say please," he replied.

I smiled indulgently. "What were you doing in the forest?"

He scowled. "What do you mean?"

ANNABEL CHASE

"Had someone alerted you to the coffin? What made you go there?"

"No," he said gruffly. "I was taking my morning walk."

His morning walk? "You walk in the woods every morning?"

"On the mornings I don't have a tee time." Sheriff Hugo was a regular on the golf course and in the local pubs. He had plenty of time for leisurely pursuits because he left the actual crime solving to everyone else.

"Do you do anything on these walks?" I asked.

He arched a bushy eyebrow. "Are you interrogating me, Miss Hart?"

I leaned back slightly. "Of course not. Just curious. I know other residents who find a walk in the woods to be good for the soul." Chief among them was Daniel.

"I usually don't see other townsfolk," the sheriff added. "I was as surprised as anyone to find a glass coffin."

"As surprised as Sophie, I imagine." I flashed a cheeky smile.

His expression clouded over. "You know the way out."

If I didn't, I had no doubt he'd be more than happy to show me.

Ginger stood in front of the class, an array of mixing bowls in front of her. "Today begins one of my favorite segments. Magical baking."

Laurel rubbed her stomach eagerly. "This was my favorite last term."

"Did anyone fail this section?" I asked in a hushed tone.

Laurel shook her head. "No, although Sophie came close. She overdid a few of the spells and disaster was narrowly avoided." Despite the pass rate, everyone had to repeat the section. A witch had to pass every class before she was

14

permitted to graduate. If she failed any one of them, then all classes had to be repeated. Rules were strict at the Arabella St. Simon Academy.

At the mention of Sophie, my expression soured. I couldn't bear to think of her rotting away in a holding cell when she didn't deserve to be there.

As though summoned by magic, Sophie burst through the door of the classroom.

"Sophie," Laurel cried.

The four of us ran to embrace her.

"I can't believe he let you out," I said, hugging her tightly.

Sophie grinned. "Apparently, the coven objected on several grounds. Lady Weatherby was very persuasive." As a member of the town council and head of the coven, Lady Weatherby wielded tremendous power in Spellbound.

"That explains why she's not here today," I said. "So are you off the hook completely?"

Sophie groaned. "Of course not. Sheriff Hugo said he'd be looking into my statement. He warned me not to leave town."

"Oh, he's hilarious," Begonia said, rolling her eyes skyward.

"Lady Weatherby is still in the sheriff's office," Sophie said. "She's trying to explain why she can't easily remove the enchantment."

"I'll bet the sheriff loves that it's complicated," I said. Sheriff Hugo wanted the easy answer to every problem. Black and white were his favorite colors.

Ginger snapped her fingers. "I know we're all thrilled to welcome Sophie back, but we need to stay on track. I don't want to be the one to tell Lady Weatherby that we fell behind her carefully set schedule."

We took our seats and watched as Ginger tapped each

bowl with her wand, filling them with a variety of ingredients.

"We'll start simple," Ginger began, "since this is all new to Emma."

Forget the magic part, baking was new to me. I wasn't exactly an expert in the kitchen, a fact that Gareth found endlessly amusing. My grandmother had considered the kitchen her domain and my grandfather and I were forbidden to enter without her explicit consent.

"Are we going to bake gingerbread surprise again?" Millie asked. Usually we weren't permitted to speak in class unless spoken to, but Ginger's style was less formal than Lady Weatherby's. One of the reasons we all liked her.

"I thought I'd vary it this term," Ginger said. "I don't want you girls getting bored."

"Do I smell honeysuckle?" Begonia asked, sniffing the air.

"You do," Ginger said. "Today we're going to learn how to bake a loaf of truth bread."

"Truth bread?" I echoed. "I thought we couldn't do spells that forced people to be truthful." I only knew because I'd asked Lady Weatherby about truth spells when I'd first arrived in Spellbound.

Ginger wagged a finger. "It's not that you can't do them," she explained. "It's that you have to be careful how much weight you place on the result. The truth can always be manipulated. Truth bread is a straightforward spell, though. Designed for simple questions, such as finding out which child spilled burstberry juice on your sofa."

As an only child, no truth spells would have been needed in my house. I was the only one to blame.

"Does the sheriff ever use truth spells?" I asked. "Like could he have Sophie eat the bread and ask her if her statement was truthful?" The magical equivalent of a lie detector test.

"The town prefers not to use magic in that way," Ginger said.

"Because there are also spells that can make you lie," Millie interjected. "What if someone had secretly used one of those? No one would know which version was the truth."

"Does truth bread always involve the same ingredients?" I asked.

Ginger shook her head. "There are always substitutions available, but you must be very careful when you use them."

"If you measure wrong or use the wrong ingredient, it changes the spell completely," Millie added.

Begonia giggled. "Remember Sophie's energy muffins?"

Sophie buried her face in her hands. "Don't remind me."

"She used the wrong ingredient and it had the opposite effect," Laurel told me. "Everyone who ate them fell asleep instead." They all began to laugh until the realization settled upon them—Sophie had used a sleeping spell once before.

"It wasn't an Endless Sleep curse," Begonia said quickly.

Sophie paled. "And it was an accident. Spell's bells, do you think the sheriff will use that as evidence against me?"

The room fell silent.

Ginger forced a bright smile. "There's no reason for anyone to mention it, is there?" She waved Sophie forward. "Come on then, Soph. You're my helper today."

Hesitantly, Sophie stood and walked to the front of the room. "Maybe this is a bad idea."

"Don't be ridiculous," Ginger assured her. "You're one of us, Sophie Gale. We're not letting anyone send you to prison."

"I feel so awful for Freddie," Sophie admitted. "Yet most of the time, I'm worried about myself. Shouldn't I be worried about him? I mean, he's the one in eternal slumber." A few tears escaped and she dabbed them away with a handy tissue.

"We all feel terribly about what's happened to Freddie,"

Ginger said, placing a comforting arm around her. "No one is going to ignore him. There are plenty of people in Spellbound who care about both of you."

Sophie mustered a smile. "I know. I'm very lucky."

"Good. While you're feeling lucky," Ginger said, "let's bake some magical bread."

I observed closely as Sophie and Ginger measured ingredients and kneaded the dough. Every single step in the instructions had to be strictly followed. There was no room for error. I felt my anxiety slowly increasing at the thought. Good thing I was still taking the anti-anxiety potion that I acquired during broomstick training. It seemed to be helping, along with harp therapy. Since I also had trouble sleeping, I started to use harp music to help me sleep at night. Gareth and Sedgwick complained bitterly, but I didn't care. I was having the best sleep of my life and I had no intention of stopping because they disliked the harp. I had a bedroom door and I wasn't afraid to use it.

"Can you use the truth ingredients in other things beside bread?" I asked.

"Absolutely," Ginger said. "You can grind them up and make a powder or liquefy them for a potion. As with many spells, there are loads of options."

A gust of air blew through the open window and Sedgwick flew into the classroom.

"Sedgwick," I chastised him. "You have to be more careful. You could have made a mess of the ingredients."

Ginger gave me a sympathetic smile. "It's fine. We're ready to bake it now."

What's so urgent? I asked.

There's a vigil later today for the dwarf, he said. *Thought you'd want to know. Maybe show up and troll for suspects.*

You're being very accommodating, I said. It was rather suspicious. Sedgwick usually preferred sarcasm to selflessness.

The sooner they wake up the dwarf, the sooner I get my forest back. All of the foot traffic coming in and out to see the coffin is scaring my food away.

Ah, now it all made sense.

Thanks for the heads up, I said. *I'll see what I can find out.*

CHAPTER 3

THE VIGIL WAS HELD at sunset. Ribbons of orange, pink and red streamed through the trees, bathing the casket in colorful light.

"He looks so peaceful," Begonia whispered. "I guess that means he's having pleasant dreams, right?"

Trust Begonia to look on the bright side of a coma.

I surveyed the attendees, trying to zero in on any potential suspects. I hadn't met Freddie yet, so many of the residents here to pay their respects were unfamiliar to me.

"Don't look now, but your neighbors are here," Millie said.

I casually turned my head in time to see the arrival of the Minors. The parade of fearsome harpies was led by Octavia, their caustic matriarch.

The visitors moved aside to let Octavia pass. She wasn't physically intimidating—not in her human form, at least—but she could crush you with a single look. Most residents were smart enough to stay off her radar.

"I haven't seen the Endless Sleep spell at work since that whiny princess back in the old kingdom," Octavia said. She stood over the glass coffin, studying the dwarf's appearance. "If anything like this ever happens to me, make sure you don't let my mustache grow in."

"I wouldn't dream of it," Marisol said, dutiful daughter that she was.

"And be sure to pluck my chin hairs. If you leave it too late, the ants will be braiding them before long."

Marisol nodded somberly.

"What would you care about facial hair when you're in an endless sleep?" Phoebe asked. Phoebe was a few years older than Marisol and just as acerbic as her mother. I'd gotten to know her a little bit in harp therapy class—well enough that I steered clear to the extent possible.

Octavia rounded on her daughter, pointing a jagged fingernail in her direction. "And that's exactly the attitude that keeps you a spinster, darling daughter."

"I'd like to say a few words, if nobody minds," a sweet voice interjected.

A young woman stepped forward. She was short and busty, with brown hair and big brown eyes. Between her sweet voice and soft demeanor, she struck me as a hugger.

"For those of you who don't know me, my name is Heidi," she said. "I've known Freddie for years."

"Heidi's a naiad," Begonia whispered. Naiads were water nymphs. "Her grandmother helped design the fountain near the town square."

"Everyone who's come into contact with Freddie is aware of his kind and generous heart," Heidi continued. "He's the type of dwarf who helps a frog across the pond when there are no lily pads. He would give you his last piece of crust if you were both starving. He's an inspiration to us all and I hope we can find a way to wake him."

Heidi's fingertips brushed against the glass coffin as she gazed wistfully at the dwarf inside. A satyr emerged from the crowd and placed a loving arm around her. She kissed her fingers and touched the glass one more time before allowing herself to be led away. I noticed the tears streaming down her cheeks as she passed by.

Another woman waddled over to the coffin and placed both hands on the side, close to where his head rested. She was too short to reach any higher.

"That's Trixie," Millie said in a hushed tone. "Freddie's sister."

Trixie said nothing as she observed her brother. There were no tears. Unlike Heidi, Trixie did not seem like much of a hugger. Not that there was anything wrong with that. Plenty of lovely people weren't inclined to give hugs. My grandmother had been one of them.

Sheriff Hugo moved closer to the coffin and turned to address the crowd. "We're doing everything we can to get to the bottom of this sad situation. If anyone has information regarding Freddie, please don't hesitate to come by the office. Even if you don't think it's relevant. If you have something to say, we want to hear it."

Well, that was more proactive than his usual lazy approach to law enforcement. Maybe the golf course was closed for repairs.

A few more people spoke, mainly co-workers from the bank where Freddie worked. I saw Heidi and the satyr heading back through the forest, so I slipped away from the vigil for a quick word.

"Heidi?"

She turned to face me, her eyes pink and puffy. "Yes?"

"You don't know me, but my name is Emma Hart."

"The new witch," the satyr said. "I'm Paul." He offered his hand and I shook it.

"You said such nice things about Freddie," I said. "It makes me sad that I haven't had the chance to get to know him yet."

"When he wakes up," she said, "you will." Her voice radiated confidence. She either truly believed he would awaken or managed to delude herself into believing it.

"I thought maybe Freddie was your boyfriend," I said. "The way you spoke about him..." My gaze flickered from Heidi to Paul.

"Oh no," Heidi said with a nervous laugh. "Freddie and I are good friends. Paul is my boyfriend."

"Yes, I realize that now. How long have you two been together?" I asked.

They smiled at each other. "It was a year last week," Paul said. "We met at the country club."

"On the golf course?" I asked.

They looked at each other and laughed.

"No," Paul said. "We both work there. Heidi runs the aquatic center and I'm a trainer."

Now Paul was a trainer I could get on board with. His goat-like lower half guaranteed no squats.

"What about Freddie?" I asked. "Did he have anyone special?"

Heidi's expression clouded over. "Not at the moment. Not for lack of trying, though."

"He was a regular at Thursday night speed dating," Paul said. "And I heard he paid a visit to Pandora, too." Pandora was a local matchmaker.

"Do you have any clue why someone would do this to him?" I asked.

Heidi shook her head. "I have to think it was a case of mistaken identity. Freddie didn't have any enemies."

Paul scrutinized me. "Sheriff Hugo arrested one of your classmates, didn't he?"

"Sophie's the one who found him," I said. "Nothing more. The sheriff had no evidence to the contrary. That's why he let her go."

Paul didn't appear convinced. "I heard a witness came forward."

That was news to me. "What witness?"

"Some wereweasel called Mike claims he saw Sophie with Freddie or something."

"Where?" I asked. "In the forest?"

"I think that's what he said."

"I thought he said it was at Thursday night speed dating," Heidi said reluctantly. I could tell she didn't want to be the bearer of bad news.

"I don't think Sophie's ever been to speed dating," I objected. "I promise you. Not only is Sophie a lovely person who would never hurt anyone, she's also a remedial witch. The Endless Sleep curse is way above her pay grade."

"Doesn't mean she didn't have help," Paul countered. "Witches tend to stick together."

Heidi patted her boyfriend's arm. "That's enough, Paul. Emma's only trying to help her friend. Freddie would do the same for me."

"I know the coven is working with Mayor Knightsbridge and Sheriff Hugo to see if they can break the spell," I said.

Heidi mustered a smile. "Yes, Lady Weatherby is very kind."

I nearly choked on my own saliva. "Yes," I managed to say. "She is." There were many adjectives to describe the head of the coven, but 'kind' was not on the list.

"Good to meet you, Emma," Heidi said, as Paul steered her away.

"Same here," I called after them.

Lucy, my fairy friend, fluttered beside me, her pink wing tickling my arm. "What are you thinking? Is Heidi a suspect?"

I stared into the darkening forest. "I don't know. She seemed genuinely upset and he seemed like a typical guy." Albeit with a goat's legs, ears, horns and a tail.

"Mayor Knightsbridge is eager to have the spell broken," Lucy said. "She doesn't like the coffin on display like this. It sets a negative tone." As the mayor's assistant, Lucy was privy to all sorts of town gossip.

"Can't say I blame her," I said. "So what do you know about Thursday night speed dating?"

Lucy perked up. "You want to try speed dating?"

"No," I said quickly, "Freddie was a regular and I want to get Sophie scratched off the list of suspects. If speed dating is the price I pay to make it happen, then so be it."

"Can I get her off the hook, too?" Lucy asked.

"The more, the merrier," I replied.

Lucy's wings beat rapidly. "We're going to have the best time."

"The best time doing what?" Begonia asked, joining us.

"We're going to speed dating on Thursday night," Lucy said.

"I'll need to miss harp therapy, though." I hated to skip a class, but at least I could still attend on Tuesday.

"Are there any hot guys in harp therapy?" Begonia asked.

"None whatsoever," I said.

Begonia pounded me between the shoulder blades. "Decision made."

"I'm not actually interested in speed dating, you know," I said. "I just need information."

"Sure," Lucy said. "Let's all go in search of information. Tall, muscular information."

"I love to get my hands on as much information as I can," Begonia said, wiggling her eyebrows.

Good grief. I had the sinking feeling that speed dating was a very, very bad idea.

. . .

Speed dating at Cupid's Arrow was like the inside of a supernatural circus tent. There were about a dozen small stations, each with two chairs and a bistro table. The female participants were instructed to start at their assigned number and work their way around the room, giving each person a chance to meet every member of the opposite sex in attendance. I assumed there wasn't a similar evening for same-sex couples. If there had been, maybe Gareth wouldn't have felt compelled to stay in the coffin for so long.

"I don't see any vampires," Begonia said, her disappointment evident.

"There's lots of male meat here," Lucy said. "You don't have to date a vampire."

Begonia pinched my arm. "Don't look now, but I see Lars."

"Who's Lars?" I asked.

"An incubus," Lucy said. She didn't look nearly as enthusiastic as Begonia.

"Speed dating must be like shooting fish in a barrel for him," I said.

Begonia's brow wrinkled. "I have no idea what that means. Why would you shoot fish in a barrel?"

"Forget it," I said, as I watched Lars roll up his sleeves and flex his biceps. *Give me strength.* "My mission here tonight is to find the wereweasel who's fabricating stories about Sophie. You girls have fun."

"No way," Begonia said. "We're here to help, too. We want Sophie exonerated as much as anyone. She's one of us."

My resolve strengthened. I'd make it through tonight for Sophie's sake. We all would.

"And if I get a good date out of it," Begonia whispered, "all the better."

A voice boomed. "Attention daters. Please take a sticker and a number from the admission table and listen for the bell. Then take your seats. You have six minutes at each table."

Suddenly, dating felt very much like school.

I took my number, slapped a sticker on my cardigan, and waited for the bell to ring. There was no mistaking the loud clanging in my ears. I glanced at my number. Six. I moved swiftly to the table, careful not to get trampled by the hooves of eager centaurs and satyrs.

Lars smiled seductively as I approached. Stars and stones, this guy wasn't wasting a precious second of his six minutes.

"You're new," he said. "I definitely would remember seeing you here."

So that line made it all the way from dive bars in the human world to the Spellbound dating scene. Some things were better left behind.

"I'm Emma. Nice to meet you." I pulled my cardigan across my chest and was careful not to flirt or smile too openly. Nothing to give him the idea that I was interested. I was biding my time for the wereweasel.

"You have the most piercing green eyes I've ever seen," he said, leaning forward to gaze at me. Despite his best efforts, his words sounded hollow to me, part of his incubus shtick. "I've never seen gold flecks like that around the iris."

"Thank you."

He leaned back against his chair, draping his arm casually along the edge of the table. "Now this is the part where you compliment me. Most ladies like to say something about my cheekbones. But I'll leave that up to you."

What a charmer. And here I thought an incubus was supposed to lure women in, not repel them. I suppose this guy relied entirely on his looks.

"I'm good. Thanks."

He looked confused. "We only have four minutes left.

Don't you want to be the one to walk out of here with me tonight?"

I choked back laughter. "Like I said, I'm good. Thanks." I hoped Begonia wasn't actually interested in Lars. This was the first real conversation I'd had with an incubus, but I refused to believe that they were all so repulsive.

Anger flashed in his eyes. "Look at this chest," he said, pounding on the taut muscle. "Women worship this. Go on. Touch it."

I snorted in a very unladylike fashion. "I'll take your word for it."

He cocked his head. "You don't want to touch it?"

"It is a very nice chest. I'm just not in the market for someone to worship right now." Truth be told, I already worshipped at the altar of a fallen angel. My mantel didn't have room for another idol.

The bell rang and the females jumped up to switch seats. The incubus remained seated, waiting for his next victim. I moved on to table seven. My next 'date' was slight in frame, with pointy ears and a friendly smile.

"Thank goodness," I breathed, as I slid into the seat.

The elf chuckled. "I take it you met Lars."

"Is he always like that?"

"Sometimes if my date isn't saying anything, I like to eavesdrop on his conversation. It passes the time."

I laughed. "I hope you don't think you're learning a thing or two from him."

"I'm learning what not to do." His pleasant expression faded. "Although he still seems to walk out of here with someone every week. So I guess it works for him."

The elf seemed sweet. "What's your name?"

"Claude. I know who you are. I think everyone in town knows who you are." He drank water from the glass on the table. "Sorry, I get parched talking at these things. Would you like a drink?"

"No, thank you."

"I imagine you'd be a fascinating person to talk to." He rested his chin on his fists. "What's it like in the human world? Do you miss it?"

"Have you ever been?" I had no clue about the lifespan of an elf. I knew they weren't immortal, but not much more than that. Another reason I needed to read up on Spellbound.

"I was born here. I've never been in the human world, but I like to read about it. Is it true that there's a body of water so wide, it takes weeks to cross it?"

Claude had never seen the ocean. Granted, I never spent time at the beach, but at least I was familiar with the planet's geography.

"The oceans are pretty big, yes. The biggest is the Pacific." It felt nice to be the knowledgeable one for a change. Usually, I felt like a toddler attending college.

"Have you been there?" he asked wistfully. "I'd like to see an ocean one day."

Unless the curse on Spellbound was ever broken, there was little chance of that.

"My family tended to avoid the ocean," I said. "My mother drowned when I was three, so bodies of water weren't in our travel plans."

He nodded gravely. "That's right. Witches can't swim." He patted my hand. "I'm sorry. That was thoughtless of me."

"Don't worry about it," I said. Claude seemed so nice and normal. Why was it difficult for him to meet someone? "I have two friends with me tonight, Lucy and Begonia. They're both great girls."

He smiled. "You're really nice, too."

Oh. I didn't want Claude to think I was interested. "Thanks. You should talk to Begonia. She's the nicest witch in our class. And Lucy is very successful. She's the assistant to the mayor."

Claude opened his mouth to say something else, but the sound of the bell cut him off. How many people here were saved by the bell every week?

"It was great to meet you, Claude. Don't be a stranger."

I got up quickly before he could say anything else and moved to table eight. The guy sitting there was not as cute as Claude, but didn't appear as obnoxious as Lars.

"Mike," he said immediately and shook my hand. "You're a witch. I can smell it."

"Yes, I'm Emma. Good to meet you. So far I've met an incubus and an elf. What can I tick off my list now?"

He smiled and his shoulders relaxed. "Wereweasel. We're not the most common or the most popular of shifters, but we're a good pack to know."

Finally. My wereweasel. I subtly adjusted my position so that I could play with my hair. According to Begonia, playing with hair was a sign of flirtation.

"I've met werewolves, a werepanther, and a wereferret, but you are definitely the first wereweasel I've met in town. Do you know Ricardo?" Ricardo was the owner of the Ready-to-Were boutique in the town square. Thanks to Lucy's impeccable taste, it was my go-to shop for clothes. Everything you tried on there fit like a glove and seemed custom-designed for your shape. It was sartorial heaven.

Mike nodded. "I see Ricardo at the pubs now and then. The wereferrets and wereweasels tend to stick together. All the smaller packs do."

I sensed resentment beneath his calm exterior. It must be difficult not being the top of the food chain. The werewolves definitely ruled Spellbound. Size and strength made sure of that.

"So Mike, how often do you come to speed dating?"

Mike gulped his ale. "As often as I can. It's hard to make time to meet someone special."

"What keeps you so busy?" I asked. "Your job?"

"That and I've tried meeting girls in the regular places, but it never seems to pan out. They're out with their friends and they don't want to be bothered or they're too shy to talk to you. I like this arrangement because we all know why we're here."

Well, he didn't know why I was here.

The minutes were ticking away. I had to make an impression so that he asked me out. I wasn't going to get the information I needed in the remaining minutes.

"I feel like I've barely scratched the surface of Spellbound," I said. "It would be nice to get to know more people. Someone friendly and willing to teach me things." That sounded lame even in my head, but it seemed to do the trick for Mike.

"I'm a pretty awesome teacher," he said, his gaze drifting to my chest. "I'd be happy to tutor you in any area you wanted."

I cringed inwardly. He gave off a slimy vibe and I was feeding right into it. I could understand why girls didn't want to speak to him voluntarily.

I glanced at the clock. One minute left. I had to close the deal.

"I'm available tomorrow night," I said, letting the offer dangle between us.

"I can't do the next couple of nights. I've got a pack meeting and then we have our weekly rodent hunting the night after."

I swallowed hard. "Night after that then?"

"I'll pick you up at seven," he said. "You live in that dead vampire's house, right?"

I bristled. "Yes, his name is Gareth." He wasn't just some

31

dead vampire. It irked me that Mike would refer to him that way. Gareth had been the public defender and a key member of the Spellbound community. No wonder Mike was marginalized. He showed no respect.

"You should ditch the cardigan, by the way," Mike said. "It makes you look uptight."

It took every ounce of strength not to give his shin a swift kick under the table. Instead, I smiled and said sweetly, "Thanks, I'll bear that in mind."

CHAPTER 4

ALTHEA TOSSED a folder onto my desk. "Hide the moonshine. You have a client coming in this afternoon."

I gave her a blank look. "I don't have any moonshine."

"No, but I do." She gestured over my shoulder. "I keep it in your office because mine gets too warm with the afternoon sun."

I whipped around and, sure enough, a silver drum was pushed against the wall. "That looks heavy."

Althea clucked her tongue as she circumvented my desk and proceeded to push the drum with ease.

"Oh, I didn't see the wheels," I said. "Who's the client?"

"His name is Thom Farley. Go easy on him. He's a nice guy."

I flipped through the folder. "What's the crime?"

"Burglary," she said. "He's allegedly been stealing from the home of his ex-girlfriend over the past month. She finally caught him."

"Caught him how?"

"She claims she saw him fleeing the house when she

arrived home early from work," Althea said. "It's all in the file."

"How do you know him?" I asked. Althea wasn't exactly bursting with praise and compliments, so if she said he was a nice guy, then he was a nice guy.

"He's a carpenter. I know him through my sister, Amanda."

"The one who makes garden gnomes?" I asked. Althea had two Gorgon sisters in Spellbound—Amanda and Miranda.

"Yes, sometimes they work on garden projects together."

"I hope I can help him," I said. I wasn't feeling very confident, not with everything happening with Sophie. I glanced at the top page. "It says he's a brownie. What is that exactly?"

"Brownies are considered a type of goblin," Althea said. "But they remind me more of leprechauns."

At the mention of 'goblin,' I shivered. Mumford was a goblin that attacked me when I first arrived in town.

Althea must've sensed my thought process because she quickly jumped in. "He's nothing like Mumford," she assured me. "Brownies are sociable and helpful. My sister can't say enough good things about Thom and she's known him for years."

I'd bear that in mind in case I needed to call a character witness. "Let me get up to speed on his case then."

She rolled the drum toward her office. "I'll leave you to it."

I relaxed when the sound of hissing snakes faded away. I didn't think I'd ever get used to my assistant's snake-covered head.

I read through Thom's file and then thumbed through the book on burglary on Gareth's bookshelf. According to the file, Thom had taken at least five items from the home of his ex-girlfriend, but none of them appeared particularly valuable. A vase, a carved horse, a T-shirt, a book of poetry, and a knitted hat. Somehow, I doubted that he intended to sell any of these items on the black market.

By the time Thom arrived, I was as up-to-date as I could be on burglary laws in Spellbound. Thom ambled into my office carrying a walking staff. He was short, although not as short as a dwarf. His chin was so long that it was practically pointy and his rosy cheeks gave him a jolly Santa Claus vibe.

"Come on in, Thom," I said, giving him a warm smile. "Have a seat."

Thom leaned his walking staff on his chair before sitting down.

"Do you actually need that staff to walk? Or is it just a fashion accessory?" I asked.

"It's the mark of a brownie," he said. "It's one way of identifying us out on the street. Most of us carry one. No real need for it other than tradition." He handed me the stick. "I carved it myself."

I touched the intricate leaf pattern on the length of wood. "It's beautiful, Thom. You're very talented."

He beamed with pride as I returned his staff.

"So I understand you've run into some trouble with the law," I said. "Care to tell me your side of the story?" I liked to hear my client's version of events in their own words. More often than not, I learned a critical fact that wasn't in the file.

"I wasn't stealing anything," he said. "It's bad enough that Lara chucked me. Now she has to go making my life miserable by accusing me of this ridiculous crime. Who steals a book?"

"Lara is your ex-girlfriend?"

He nodded and a shadow passed across his jolly features. "Together for two years, we were. Happy as two horns on a minotaur's head."

"So what happened?"

His pointy jaw tensed. "One day, out of the blue, she told

me she didn't love me anymore. That she was sorry, but the relationship was over. Just like that." He snapped his fingers. "Can you imagine saying that to someone you spent the last two years of your life with?"

I couldn't, but then again, I'd never been in a serious relationship. "Was there an inciting incident? A big fight that precipitated the breakup or maybe someone else?"

He grunted. "There's someone else for her now, although she swears he wasn't in the picture when she dumped me."

"So if she broke up with you, why would she lie about you stealing from her? What purpose does it serve?"

He stroked his chin. "Who knows? Lara tended to be emotional. She's a pixie, after all. They're known for their tempers."

That was the first time someone mentioned a pixie's temper. I'd have to confirm the information.

"The only way it makes sense to me that she falsely accused you is if you'd done something to cause the breakup," I said. "If she broke up with you in anger, then I could understand her need for some kind of revenge." Although it seemed to me she could've done better than the items listed in the file. Could she not have accused him of stealing jewelry or something of value?

"I work a lot of hours. She was always complaining about the fact that I wasn't around enough."

"You have your own carpentry business, right?"

He nodded. "It's my passion. I love to work with my hands and build things from scratch. There's no substitute for working with wood. You can make miracles with it." I heard the note of pride in his voice and it warmed me. It was encouraging when people took pride in their work.

"What types of things do you make? Furniture?"

"I'll take on commission projects. Someone will ask me for a certain sized table or a chair. They might request that it look a certain way. The best days are when I get to do my own creations. I love having a vision and carving it into reality."

"I can see why you spend so much time at your job," I said. "What does Lara do?"

"She's a teacher at the local high school."

"Which subject does she teach?"

"English literature," he replied.

"It says in the file that one of the items you stole was a book of poetry. Do you know anything about that?"

"Do I look like the type of guy who recites poems?" he asked. "I work with my hands. I don't go in for that namby-pamby stuff. That's all Lara."

So Thom was jolly but not romantic. Got it. "Then how do you explain the fact that the sheriff found these items in your house."

The rose of his cheeks deepened. "I don't know how they got there. Lara must've snuck into my house when I wasn't home and hidden them to frame me."

"Who's her new boyfriend?"

"Some yokel at the high school. Another teacher." He shuddered. "He teaches physical education. Can you imagine? She'd rather be with someone who blows a whistle for a living than with someone who creates art. I can't believe I never realized how shallow she is."

Okay, maybe Thom was more romantic than I'd given him credit for. "Do you know the gym teacher's name?"

"He's a nymph called Petros. Guy even has a beard. How do you go from skin as smooth as a baby's bum to one as scratchy as a hestleberry bush?"

"I don't know, Thom. How about you? Have you met anyone new?"

Thom folded his arms. "Absolutely not. I'm sticking with my one true love. Woodworking. I spend more time in my workshop now than I did when I was with Lara and I love every minute of it."

He was hurt badly. I got the sense that his workshop served as a retreat from the world. Sadly, I understood the impetus all too well. After my father died, I wanted to spend all my free time in my bedroom. My grandparents forced me to go to school, but they couldn't get me to do much else. It took a long time for me to want to reengage with the world.

"I'm sure you already know this, but there's speed dating every Thursday at Cupid's Arrow. Maybe you'd consider showing up one night." I didn't want Thom to waste his life wallowing in self-pity.

"I think it's best to wait until after this trial, don't you?" He grinned at me. "Unless you're that confident in your skills."

"Fair enough. How about we make a deal? If I manage to keep you out of prison, then you'll agree to give speed dating a try."

He stood and shook my hand. "Miss Hart, you have yourself a deal."

"I don't know why I let you talk me into this," I said.

Although Lars didn't leave with Begonia the night of speed dating, he did ask her out to dinner. She was too nervous to go alone, so she convinced me to join them. I had a hard time saying no to Begonia's puppy dog eyes. I invited Claude to come along since he was the nicest guy I met at speed dating, though I tried to make it clear from the outset that he was strictly in the friend zone.

"Because you're a good friend," Begonia whispered, as the hostess seated us.

Dragon's Lair was a quaint restaurant tucked down a side street near the town square. The interior had an Asian vibe with splashes of red and gold and a mural of dragons on the wall. I was relieved to see that many of the menu choices were familiar. Sometimes I felt like Spellbound menus required a translator.

"I hear you're defending Thom Farley," Claude said.

"I am. Do you know him?"

"A little," Claude replied. "He made a crib for my nephew. My brother and his wife raved over it."

Lars scrunched his nose at the mention of a crib. "Babies are the kiss of death for a relationship."

Begonia inclined her head. "How can you say that? I know lots of happily married couples with kids. My parents are just as in love today as the day they married."

"That's what they want you to think," Lars said. "I guarantee you they're looking sideways at other people."

I couldn't tell whether this was a general incubus attitude or the world according to Lars.

"I'm with Begonia," Claude said. "My parents are together and my brother and his wife are very happy. If anything, their baby brought them closer together."

Lars stuck his nose in the menu, effectively tuning us out.

"What about your parents?" Claude asked me. "Are they together?"

Emotions stirred within me. It was difficult to talk about my parents at the best of times. "They were definitely happy together."

"Emma's mom died when she was little," Begonia said.

Claude smacked his forehead. "Dragons alive, you told me that. How stupid of me. It must have been hell for you and your dad."

"If it hadn't been for me, I don't think my father would have made an effort to get up in the mornings." And sometimes he didn't.

"Did he remarry?" Claude asked.

I shook my head. "He died when I was seven. I was raised by his parents."

Claude whistled softly. "I'm sorry. I didn't realize."

"That's okay. I know it's hard to say for sure, but I bet they'd still be together today, had they lived." I truly believed that.

"Does everyone know what they want?" Lars asked.

"I'm ready," Begonia said.

Lars tapped his menu and I realized it was the same magical ordering system as Moonshine, a restaurant I'd visited with Demetrius. We tapped our menu items and the order was transmitted to the kitchen.

"What did you order?" Begonia asked Lars.

"A roasted chicken sprinkled with pixie dust. It gives it that extra kick. I don't like it bland."

I was still on the fence. "How about you, Begonia?"

"Prime rib cooked rare."

Out of the corner of my eye, I noticed the incubus stiffen. Claude and I placed our orders at the same time, while Lars excused himself to use the restroom.

"He's super cute, right?" Begonia asked, once he was gone.

"Absolutely," I said. He wasn't my type, but I could see the allure.

"He must like you," Claude said to Begonia. "It seems to me he usually doesn't make much of an effort."

We continued to chat and our drinks floated over within ten minutes. By the time our meals arrived, Lars still had not returned.

"Do you think he's ill in the bathroom?" I asked. I looked at Claude. "Would you mind checking on him?"

"No problem," he said. He returned after a few minutes, frowning. "He's not in there."

Begonia and I exchanged surprised looks. Her cheeks reddened and I was fairly certain she was about to cry.

"Stay here," I said. "I'll go look for him."

"Don't be silly," Begonia objected. "He's my date. I should look for him."

"But your dinner tastes better warm. Mine doesn't matter." I smiled. "I'll be right back. I promise."

I hurried from the restaurant and looked up and down the cobblestone street for any sign of the incubus. As I was straining to see in the darkness, I heard a familiar voice.

"Emma, what are you doing out here?"

I turned to see Lucy, her pink wings glowing in the darkness. "I'm looking for Lars. He was having dinner with us, but he disappeared."

"I don't suppose you have your broomstick with you," Lucy said.

I placed a hand on my hip. "It's past sundown, so I'm not allowed to fly. Not that I would anyway. You know how I feel about that."

Lucy giggled. "Sorry, I keep thinking you'll grow out of it. If you want, I can do a quick zip around the block."

"That would be great. Begonia is inside eating dinner and I know she's concerned."

"Be back in a jiffy." Lucy's wings increased speed tenfold and she was gone in a flash. She returned three minutes later, gripping Lars under the shoulders and dropping him at my feet. I couldn't help but laugh. The petite fairy had the strength of a dozen men.

"He wasn't planning to come back," Lucy said, giving him a dirty look. "Why don't you tell Emma what you told me?"

Lars pulled himself to his feet and raked his fingers through his slick hair. "I was trying to be nice about it."

"You ran off into the night in the middle of the date," I said heatedly. "On what planet is that being nice?"

Lars scoffed at me. "I didn't want to humiliate her."

"What did I miss? The date seemed to be going well."

"It was, until she ordered prime rib. And rare." He shuddered.

"You're a vegetarian?" I queried.

"No, I love prime rib, but it's so unattractive for her to want it. And to order it rare? She may as well be a vampire." He made a slicing gesture with his arm. "Complete turnoff."

So Lars had very specific ideas about women. "You don't just abandon someone in the middle of a date," I said. "Begonia had no idea why you left."

"I'll let you tell her," he said. "I spotted a hot pixie around the block before I was snatched up by psychofairy here." He jerked his chin toward Lucy. "I'll bet you twenty gold coins I won't see her ordering prime rib."

He stalked off and Lucy gave me a questioning look. "Do you want me to go after him?"

I shook my head. "Begonia is better off. I'll explain it to her." With kid gloves.

When I returned to the table, Begonia and Claude were so deep in conversation, they barely noticed my arrival.

Begonia blinked at me, finally registering my presence. "Did you find him?"

"I did. Turns out he wasn't feeling well," I lied. I had to spare her feelings. "It doesn't matter, though. He's not the guy for you."

I felt Begonia's foot press on top of mine. "I really need the restroom. You need to go to, don't you?"

I took the pressure of her foot as a sign that I did, indeed, need to go too.

We pushed back our chairs. "Be back in a minute," I said. "Sorry."

Begonia tucked her arm through mine and guided me to the restroom. Once we were safely behind closed doors, she whipped around and grabbed me by the shoulders. "How much do you like your date? You don't really like him, do you? Because you not-so-secretly like Daniel, right?"

I shook my head. "Whoa, Begonia. Slow down. What's the matter? Was he rude while I was looking for Lars?"

Her expression turned dreamy. "Not at all. Actually, we were having a really great conversation about our cats. Turns out he loves cats." She hesitated. "I'm thinking...Is it okay if I go out with him another time?"

It took a moment for me to register her request. She was asking to date my date. I broke into a broad smile.

"Holy date stealer, I would absolutely love it if you went out with him. He seems really nice." In truth, I was overjoyed. I had no interest in Claude, and Begonia had quickly become one of my best friends. "By all means, date, get married, have many babies. Thom will make you a crib. You have my blessing."

Begonia squealed and pinched the skin on my arms. "Thank you so much. You're the best."

I glanced at the empty stalls. "We don't really need to use the restroom, do we?"

Begonia shrugged. "We may as well, since we're here."

Female logic. There was nothing like it.

CHAPTER 5

I CHOSE the next afternoon to follow up on Maeve's suggestion and speak with Agnes, the former head of the coven. My palms were sweaty on the wheel as I drove Sigmund across town to the Spellbound Care Home. The home was on the outskirts of town, past the church and the Mayor's Mansion to the east. The building was nondescript, especially compared with the charming nature of the downtown area. It reminded me of drab 1970's architecture. For the sake of the inhabitants, I hoped the interior was more cheerful.

I plucked the bag of chocolates and the bottle of Fangtastic from the passenger seat and headed inside. A young pixie greeted me from behind the reception desk. She looked like a fairy, except her wings were smaller and her ears were slightly pointed like an elf's.

"Hello, my name is Emma Hart. I'm the new public defender in town."

The pixie brightened. "Oh my gosh. You're the new witch! I can't believe it. This is so exciting."

It wasn't the first time I'd felt like a celebrity in Spellbound.

"A member of the council suggested that I come here to speak with Agnes," I said. "Is she available?"

The pixie frowned. "We don't normally let unrelated visitors through without the consent of the resident."

"Does Agnes ever have any visitors? I was under the impression that she had no family members." I sighed deeply. "I guess that will be me someday. Cut off from society because I have no family. It's tragic, really."

Although I was exaggerating for the pixie's benefit, there was a ring of truth to my statement. I had no family in Spellbound. Unless I eventually married and had children, the Spellbound Care Home *was* my future. It was a sobering thought.

The pixie cast a furtive glance around the lobby. No one else was within earshot.

"She's in room 151," the pixie whispered. "Be careful with her, though. She may be old, but she's sharp as a vampire's fang."

"Thank you so much. I really appreciate it."

The pixie buzzed me in and I walked through the barrier and down the long corridor until I reached room 151. The door was ajar, but I decided to knock anyway. If she wasn't accustomed to visitors, I had no clue what state I'd find her in.

"Go away, Silas," a voice croaked. "If I've told you once, I've told you a million times, I am not interested in your man parts today."

I poked my head inside. "Um, excuse me. Are you Agnes?"

The old woman sat at a table beside her bed. She was in the middle of dealing cards. Magical solitaire? The cards were different than anything I'd ever seen. Instead of jacks, kings, and queens, there were werewolves, vampires, and witches.

The old woman studied me carefully. "Who are you? You don't work here."

"No, I'm a visitor."

"Then what are you doing in here? Get on with your visit." She turned her attention back to her cards.

"Actually, I'm here to visit you. Maeve McCullen recommended that I speak with you."

That seemed to get her attention. She leaned back in her chair. "The banshee sent you, eh? And why should I speak with you?"

I held up the bottle of Fangtastic and shook the bag of chocolates. "I come bearing gifts."

Her wrinkled face produced a smile. Her teeth were yellowed and pointy. She reminded me of the old witch in the forest, the one you imagined trying to eat Hansel and Gretel—very unlike the elegant yet intimidating Lady Weatherby.

"How did you manage to sneak those in?" She eyed me with a mixture of admiration and suspicion.

"To be honest, I'm a little bit of a celebrity in town. I just walked in with them."

"A celebrity, eh?" She tapped her long and twisted fingernails on the table. The sound made my skin crawl, but I remained still, wanting to win her approval. If she was the person who had information on my background, then I needed to do whatever it took to get her to open up.

"Set them here," she said.

"Not until you've answered a few of my questions," I said. If she was as wily as everyone said, I wasn't about to hand over the contraband without getting a few answers first.

The old witch chuckled. "All right then. What is it that

you need to know? I'm guessing it has something to do with your coven."

My eyebrows shot up. She could tell I was from a different coven just by looking at me? Maybe she really would have answers.

"How do you know I'm from a different coven?" I asked.

"We hear the local gossip. We're not deaf." She paused. "Well, I suppose some of us are."

Okay, so her powers of observation were not as shrewd as I thought.

"Did you know I was the former head of the Spellbound coven?" Agnes pushed herself to a standing position and hobbled over to the kitchenette.

"Yes," I said. "Before Lady Weatherby."

Agnes grunted. "Cindy Ruth," she muttered. "Never saw that one coming." She pulled two shot glasses from the cabinet and set them on the counter. "You pour."

"The bottle is for you," I said. "I don't need any." Not to mention that I had no idea what Fangtastic was. I got the sense that it was comparable to whiskey or tequila. The magical hard stuff.

Agnes focused her attention fully on me for the first time. Her eyes glittered like onyx. "If I say you drink, you drink. Would you dare to question commands from Lady Weatherby?"

I shuddered at the thought. "No, definitely not." I twisted off the lid and poured the clear liquid into the glasses.

"For every answer I give you, we each do a shot," she told me.

If I didn't want to leave the care home wasted, then I needed to choose my questions carefully.

"Set the bag of chocolates here," she said, tapping her grotesque fingernails on the countertop.

I placed the bag as instructed. "What can you tell me about my coven?"

"I don't know which one your coven is," she said. "But I knew straight away that you weren't one of ours."

"How?"

She lifted the shot glass to her lips and drained it. "Drink first."

Damn. I had to be smarter about this. I tipped back the glass and felt the liquid pass down my throat. It was bitter on my tongue. The burn didn't begin until it reached my stomach. It was much stronger than anything I'd tasted in Spellbound so far.

"You don't drink much, do you?" Agnes asked with a cackle. "I do miss it. Tell me, do you spend any time at the Horned Owl?"

"I haven't been in town very long, but I've been there a few times. It's popular with the coven."

"And who do you think started that trend?" She brought the bottle and the two glasses over to her small table and settled back in her chair. She motioned for me to sit opposite her.

"How can you tell that I'm not from your coven?" I asked, seating myself in the empty chair.

"While many of my senses have dulled with age, my sense of smell remains strong. You don't smell like us, but I can tell that you're a witch." She refilled the glasses and we drank again.

"Do you know anything about a coven with owls as familiars? Or one where the witches can see ghosts?"

Agnes held up two fingers. "Two questions yield two answers."

I slumped in my chair. There was no way I was walking out of here on two feet. I hoped the floors were clean.

"I'm not familiar with a coven that sees ghosts, but I do

remember hearing about one with owls." She peered at me from beneath her wrinkled brow. "These are two of your abilities?"

I nodded. "My familiar is an owl called Sedgwick. And I can see the ghost of a vampire. I live in his house now."

"Have you seen any other ghosts?" she asked.

"No, and Gareth and I are just figuring out what his limitations are. We thought he was limited to the house, but it turns out he can also go to his old office where I work."

She waved a dismissive hand. "I'm not interested in the ghost. I am, however, interested in you." She began to shuffle the deck of cards in front of her. "Choose six cards from the deck. Turn them over in front of you."

I selected six random cards and placed them face up in front of me. "Is this some kind of psychic reading?"

"These are not tarot cards, if that's what you mean."

At that moment, a man drifted into the room. I say drifted because his bottom half was like an apparition, whereas the top half was fully formed.

"A visitor, Agnes? Tartarus must be freezing over about now."

Agnes scowled in his direction. "Go away, Silas. I'm entertaining company and you were not invited."

Silas came closer, ignoring her. "She's reading your cards?" He sounded surprised. "She must really like you."

"You're not welcome here," Agnes said.

He winked at her. "That's not what you said the other night. As I recall, you welcomed me very enthusiastically."

I bit back a smile. So Agnes had a friendly side after all.

"If I had my wand, you'd be a toad by now," she replied.

"And then the only way to return me to my princely form would be to kiss me." He puckered his lips and made a kissing sound. "I bet you'd like that."

"I'm warning you, Silas. Get your genie butt out of here

before I shove you inside the nearest lamp." She gave him a pointed look. "And I won't be rubbing it."

"Ouch." He clutched his chest.

I glanced at the cards in front of me. A werewolf, a vampire, a witch, an owl, the sun, and an angel.

"Interesting," Agnes murmured.

Silas turned his attention to me. "No one ever comes to see Agnes. What brings you here?"

"None of your business," Agnes snapped.

He spotted the bottle of Fangtastic on the table. "You naughty girls. Am I going to have to report you?"

"You know where the glasses are," Agnes said, her gaze pinned on the cards.

Silas went to the cabinet and retrieved another shot glass. He drifted over to the table and poured himself a drink. "Salut." He raised the glass to us before downing it.

"Good stuff, isn't it?" Agnes asked.

"Proof that she likes me," he told me. "She guards alcohol the way a dragon guards treasure."

"The girl brought me chocolates too, but you'd be a fool to think I'd share those with you."

"Oh, I can think of a few things I do that might encourage you to share."

I desperately wanted to cover my ears. If he started going into detail, I might have to cut my losses and run.

The door pushed open and a dwarf floated in on a chair—more of a magic carpet than a wheelchair.

"Estella," Silas said. "Join the party."

Agnes rolled her eyes. "You like this, don't you? Three nubile women and you."

Looking at the two elderly women, Agnes clearly had a different definition of nubile than I did.

Estella's eyes widened at the sight of Fangtastic. "Hallelu-jah. I could really use a shot right now."

"Go on," Silas urged softly. "We know you're worried about Freddie."

At the mention of Freddie, my ears perked up. I glanced at Estella. She looked very much like the dwarf in the glass coffin.

Silas retrieved another glass and poured a drink for the elderly dwarf.

"No amount of alcohol can dull the pain," Estella said.

"Then why bother?" Agnes queried. The old witch clearly did not want to share.

Estella swallowed the shot and handed the glass back to Silas. "Thank you. I really needed that."

"Were you at the vigil?" I asked. I was pretty sure I would have noticed a dwarf in a magical wheelchair.

Estella shook her head. "No, I'm not permitted to leave the premises."

"Her heart is too weak," Silas explained. "She very much wanted to be there. A few of the healers had to restrain her."

Estella sniffed. "Freddie is such a good boy. I can't imagine why anyone would do this to him."

"When's the last time you saw him?" I asked.

Estella looked thoughtful. "He came twice a week. The last time I saw him was a Wednesday. He came for his usual afternoon visit."

"I loved hearing his stories about the dating scene," Silas said. "I wish speed dating had been around when I was younger."

"Trust me, Silas. There's nothing speedy about you," Agnes said.

Silas chuckled. "You always say you like it slow."

Agnes unwrapped a bar of chocolate and broke off a square before eating it.

"Did you notice anything unusual about Freddie when he was here?" I asked. "Was he upset about anything?"

"No," Estella replied. "He said he met someone recently and they had their first date planned for over the weekend. He seemed pleased."

"Did he mention the name of his date?" I wondered if the sheriff had even bothered to speak with Freddie's mother.

"He didn't tell me her name, but that's typical of Freddie. He doesn't want me asking about a girl every time he visits. He knows how much I want to meet my grandbabies before I die."

Silas gently touched her shoulder. "Don't talk like that, Estella. Your heart may be weak, but your spirit is strong."

"You know I've started to eat my pudding before my dinner?" Estella said. "Just in case I don't make it to the end of the meal."

"You can't think like that," Silas said. "You have years ahead of you."

"Don't listen to a word he says, Estella," Agnes said. "He's just trying to get under your cloak."

Silas smirked. "Worked on you."

"Freddie did mention that she was a fairy," Estella said.

"Ah, fairies," Silas said. "I once had an affair with the most beautiful fairy. It was a whirlwind romance. The kind that wasn't meant to last."

The wistful expression on his face made me think of Daniel. I buried the feeling before Agnes sensed my weakness. Just because she couldn't read minds didn't mean she couldn't read *me*.

"Thank you, Estella. That's helpful information." Knowing the type of creature I was looking for narrowed the pool significantly. "A fairy shouldn't be too difficult to spot at speed dating." They were among the easiest residents to pinpoint.

"Oh," Estella said. "I don't think he met this one at speed dating. I think she was through the matchmaker."

"You know, the girl is actually here to ask me questions. Not to converse with the likes of you two." Agnes slid the bottle closer to her and I realized that she was angling for more shots. She'd made her rules and she was sticking to them.

"Come along, Estella," Silas said, pretending to pout. "If you want us, we'll be in the cafeteria."

"It'll be a cold day in Tartarus before I want you again," Agnes said.

Silas glided over to kiss her forehead before leaving. "I'll see you tonight."

"Ten o'clock," she snapped. "Don't be late."

I waited until Estella and Silas left the room to ask the question that had been burning my brain. I was just tipsy enough to ask. "Agnes, if he is incorporeal from the waist down, how do you...?"

She wiggled her gray eyebrows. "You'd be surprised what a genie is capable of." She poured two more drinks. "That counts as an answer, by the way."

I groaned. "You need to answer my questions about the coven," I insisted. "General questions shouldn't count."

Agnes shrugged. "Then you should have specified that in the beginning." She tipped back her glass and sucked down the clear liquid.

"Is there anyone else I might be able to speak with about covens besides you?" Maybe there was even someone else in the care home.

"Have you gone to see Raisa?" the old woman asked.

"Who's Raisa?" I asked.

She frowned. "So no one has mentioned her." She clucked her tongue. "I suppose I shouldn't be surprised. Raisa wanted to be forgotten. Now she is."

"Why would I want to see her?"

"You came to see me because I'm old and remember

things." She threw back her head and cackled. "Well, Raisa is even older and, as far as I know, still in possession of an excellent memory. If you have questions, she's your best chance to have them answered."

I hadn't heard of Raisa. Then again, no one had mentioned Agnes either. "Where does she live?"

"A cottage deep in the forest. If you travel north, you'll see a path where the forest meets the base of the hills. The path will lead you to her."

"Is she a witch?"

The old woman's hand shook as she tucked a limp piece of hair behind her ear. "Oh, yes. Much older than me."

"Was she ever the head of the coven?" It was hard to imagine anyone other than the intimidating Lady Weatherby in charge of the Spellbound witches.

Her lips curled into a cryptic smile. "You'll have to ask her." She poured more liquid into the glasses, spilling a few drops on the table and wiping them away with her fingers. I wasn't surprised to see her tongue dart out to lick her fingertips.

I drank again and watched with blurred vision as she poured the remainder of the bottle into the glasses. My head was spinning. There was no way I could drive Sigmund home. I'd have to call someone to collect me.

"Excuse me," I said, burping. "I need the bathroom."

"Be my guest," she said, and pointed to a door in the corner of the room.

I stumbled my way to the door, tripping over the bed as I went. At this rate, I'd be sliding out the front door on my stomach. Agnes: one, Emma: zero.

I gripped the handle on the door and tried to steady myself. My stomach churned and I realized I was about to lose my lunch. I dropped to my knees in front of the toilet and flipped up the lid just in time. Could there possibly be a week in Spellbound when I didn't vomit? I remained on the floor for a few minutes, trying not to imagine the magical germs swirling around me right now. The mere thought would have me vomiting again.

I dragged myself to the sink and rinsed my face and mouth before opening the door. The room was empty.

"Agnes?" I called. No answer.

I heard a commotion down the hall and instinctively reached for my wand, but it wasn't there.

Uh oh.

I hugged the wall as I attempted to make my way down the corridor. I was in no condition to wrestle with a wily old witch, but I had no choice. I rounded the corner in time to see her using my wand to wrap toilet paper around the assistant healers' station. It didn't help that the assistant healers were actually seated there while it was happening.

"Agnes," one of the assistant healers cried. "Please stop. We do not want to be mummies."

Agnes waved my wand menacingly. "I told you before. You will call me Lady Sparkles."

Lady Sparkles? Spell's bells, she was out of control. I watched as she ran up the side of the wall and onto the ceiling. She crouched above our heads like a creepy demon, cackling with glee.

I raced down the corridor and confronted her. "Agnes," I shouted.

"She's Lady Sparkles," one of the assistant healers hissed.

I cleared my throat and adopted my firmest tone. "Lady Sparkles. Hand over Tiffany."

Agnes turned her attention to me. "Who in the hell is Tiffany?"

"My wand."

"What kind of weirdo witch names her wand?"

"No one bats an eye at wings or horns, but I'm a nutball

for naming my wand?" Why did everyone think it was so strange to name inanimate objects? This was a town of paranormals, for crying out loud.

"You'll have to get Tiffany from me, won't you?" She dangled the wand from her place on the ceiling, taunting me.

For once, I appreciated Lady Weatherby's regal aura. I couldn't imagine her tormenting me like this. Her methods of torture were very, very different.

"Lady Sparkles, get down here this instant and give me back my wand or I will report you to the coven." Now there was a real threat.

The old witch dropped to the floor and landed on her feet. She'd learned something from her familiar over the years. I wondered where the cat was now, probably long dead.

"If you want this wand, you need to take it," Agnes said. She whirled around and pointed the wand at the assistant healers. "Stop bringing me juice in the morning. I have told you a hundred times, I detest juice."

The two women wrapped in toilet paper nodded vigorously.

"No more juice," came a muffled voice.

"These women take care of you," I said. "Show some compassion."

"I'd rather show my sense of fun," Agnes said. "It's much more interesting." She bounded down the hall with the energy of a fifteen-year-old. How could this be the feeble old woman I met an hour ago?

As if reading my mind, one of the assistant healers said to me, "It's your wand. It's feeding her magical energy. You need to stop her."

"How? She has my wand." Then I remembered something I learned from Lady Weatherby. The wand wasn't always necessary to perform a spell. Could I possibly use a spell on Agnes without my wand? I had to try.

I ventured down the hall, feeling dizzier with each step I took.

"Lady Sparkles," I called. "You're going to regret making a mess of the place where you live."

I made it to the cafeteria in time to see Agnes turn an entire table of elderly residents into frogs. They began hopping every which way, over the table and onto the plates. This was a disaster. I watched as she turned the next table into snakes. The remaining residents screamed and did their best to run out of the room. The problem was, of course, that most of them were relatively immobile. The centaur with the walker didn't stand a chance. He morphed into a snake and coiled around the leg of the metal frame, too frightened to slither.

I faced Agnes and focused my will on her. I kept my eyes open and extended my arms. "Why must she be so much trouble/Put this old witch in a bubble."

A flexible force field appeared around Agnes. She pushed around the soft edges to no avail. "Let me out."

"No. Not until you reverse the spells you've done."

Agnes glared at me. "I can't use magic inside the bubble."

"Yes, you can. Do it now."

She grunted in frustration before turning her attention to the reptiles and amphibians in the cafeteria. Although I couldn't hear the reversal spell, I saw the evidence of it as residents returned to their proper forms. When the last toad disappeared, I focused my will again.

"Tiffany," I called. "To me."

My wand slipped out of Agnes's grip, bursting the bubble in the process. It shot across the room and into my outstretched hand.

Agnes stared at me, gobsmacked. "How did you do that?"

ANNABEL CHASE

I had no idea. "Weirdo witches have all sorts of powers you don't understand."

Agnes sank into the nearest chair, seemingly exhausted without the energy from the wand. Security rushed over to restrain her.

"Promise me you'll come again soon," Agnes called. "And bring another bottle of Fangtastic."

Only in her demented dreams.

CHAPTER 6

THE STERN EXPRESSION on Lady Weatherby's face told me that today's class would not be fun and games. Not that it ever was when the head of the coven was teaching, but the glint in her steely eyes suggested a more serious agenda.

"In light of recent events, I have decided that today's class will focus on psychology," she announced.

Psychology? That was a sharp left turn from the usual curriculum.

Millie raised her hand and Lady Weatherby nodded for her to speak. "We didn't study psychology last term."

Lady Weatherby scowled. "Thank you, Millie. I am quite familiar with the covenant curriculum."

"So when you say recent events, do you mean Emma's arrival?" Millie asked.

"In truth, I was referring to a more recent incident." She paused and directed her attention to me. "It occurred at the Spellbound Care Home. A dangerous witch was given access to a wand. Only luck determined the happy outcome."

Luck, my ass. I worked some serious magic in that care home, not that she'd give me any credit.

No one dared to look in my direction. Everyone knew this latest lesson had something to do with me.

"Psychology is the study of behavior and the mind. It can play an important role in how we deal with other supernatural creatures within our town borders, especially those who are a menace to society." Lady Weatherby clasped her hands in front of her. "For example, had a certain witch been aware that Agnes was well known for manipulation and mayhem, she may opted to handle the situation differently."

My hand shot into the air. Despite my fear of Lady Weatherby, I felt an overwhelming urge to defend myself.

"Imagine that," Lady Weatherby said. "Miss Hart has something to say on the matter."

"A member of the town council suggested that I speak with Agnes. If she were so dangerous, then maybe the council member should have been the one to advise the innocent witch that the meeting came fraught with certain dangers. Furthermore, Agnes lives in a care home, not a prison. She's hardly a menace to society."

Lady Weatherby fixed her gaze on me and a shiver ran down my spine. She may as well have snapped a leather belt in my face.

"Agnes is not a menace to society as long as she does not have access to magic. Had the witch in question been better informed, she would have known to leave her wand behind. As it happens, she did not consult with the relevant witches before foolishly deciding to take it upon herself to visit the former head of the coven. Security should have known better than to let you pass without removing any magical items."

Lady Weatherby seemed uncharacteristically emotional. Even when she was upset, she typically remained cool and collected. Today, however, I was beginning to see cracks in her smooth veneer.

"If she's not in prison and has committed no crime, why is she not allowed access to magic?" I asked.

"Even the best witches can succumb to human frailties," Lady Weatherby explained. "Agnes has moments of lucidity, but she also suffers from dementia. Trust me, you do not want a magic wand in the hands of someone who forgets her own name half the time."

Agnes suffered from dementia? I never would have guessed it. She seemed wily and lucid in my presence. Still, Lady Weatherby's strong reaction surprised me.

"So is it her dementia that makes her manipulative or was that always part of her personality?" I asked.

Lady Weatherby's expression hardened. "She has always been a manipulative old woman. The dementia only makes it worse."

Mixed in with her anger, I also detected what I could only interpret as sadness.

"So if she was the former head of the coven, did you take control directly after her?" I asked. During our conversation, Agnes had seemed miffed by Lady Weatherby's rise to power. She'd even used Lady Weatherby's given name—Cindy Ruth —which Gareth had told me was a great secret.

"It was as surprising to me as to anyone when the ritual revealed my leadership role," Lady Weatherby said. "A coven does not typically pass from mother to daughter."

I froze. Mother to daughter? My head swiveled in both directions, looking for confirmation from my classmates. Did everyone know that Agnes was Lady Weatherby's mother? The only expression of surprise was on my own face. Talk about a bombshell.

"I'm sorry," I said. "Did you just say that Agnes is your mother?" In some ways, it explained so much.

"Indeed," Lady Weatherby said crisply. "Prior to me, *she*

was known as Lady Weatherby. Stripped of her title, however, she reverts to Agnes once again."

I mean, I always knew that Lady Weatherby had a mother and father because…well, biology, but it was hard to imagine the partnership that spawned the witch in front of me.

"Do you ever visit her?" I asked. Based on my interaction with Agnes, I was pretty sure I already knew the answer.

"That's none of your business," she snapped. "Not that it matters. When the person you're visiting doesn't even recognize you, there isn't much point."

"With all due respect, Lady Weatherby," I said. "You recognize her. Isn't that enough?"

Lady Weatherby brushed my comment aside. "Let's get on with the lesson, shall we? Now witches, we will begin by learning the two primary theoretical perspectives."

My thoughts drifted away as she droned on about functionalism and structuralism. I thought about my relationship with my grandmother. Had I been lucky enough to see her into old age, I would have visited her as often as possible. Time was fleeting, although I suppose life in Spellbound created a different set of expectations. Agnes could be in that care home for decades. In moments like this, I could understand Daniel's angst. Lady Weatherby didn't appreciate the time with her mother because she had all the time in the world. The parameters were different from those in the human world.

Despite Lady Weatherby's claims of manipulative behavior, it made me sad to think of Agnes alone in the care home. Okay, Agnes was scary and more than a little crazy, but I glimpsed that fun side of her. And she was smart. She still had a lot to offer the residents of Spellbound. I decided right then and there that I would visit her again, although I wouldn't be so foolish as to bring my wand. Or hard alcohol.

Maybe just a small bottle of wine for me.

. . .

Mike the wereweasel stood on my front porch at quarter to seven.

"Mike, you're early," I said as brightly as I could. Good thing I wasn't invested in the date or I'd have been mortified.

"I figured you'd be pumped for the night to start," Mike said.

Yes, pumped. "Thank you. Won't you come in?"

He gave me a surprised look. "You're inviting me in already?"

Beside me, Gareth groaned. "Devil below. This guy is such a loser."

I did my best to ignore Gareth. If Mike had information about Sophie, then I needed to hear it. I couldn't end the date before it even began.

"Just for a few minutes, while I finish getting ready."

Mike entered the foyer and looked me over. "You look good and ready to me."

"Stars and stones," Gareth complained. "Is that his attempt at sexy talk? Make it stop."

Magpie rushed onto the scene and skidded to a halt at Mike's feet. The wereweasel jumped back at the sight of the hairless wonder with a half-chewed ear.

"Snake on a stick," he cried. "What is that?"

I picked up Magpie and cuddled him, praying that he didn't bite off a chunk of my face in the process. "This is my precious cat, Magpie. I hope you like cats because he's very special to me."

Gareth choked back laughter.

"Oh, I love cats," Mike said unconvincingly. I wasn't sure what the relationship was between weasels and cats. I'd have to ask Gareth when we were alone.

I rubbed my face against Magpie's body and instantly

regretted it. My skin began to burn from the rough surface. I placed him quickly on the floor before he decided to show his true colors.

"Let me run upstairs and I'll be ready to go," I said. I raced up the steps to my bedroom to grab the packet of truth powder Sophie had acquired for me. Gareth beat me there.

"Oh, how I wish I could accompany you this evening," he said, overflowing with giddy energy. "I haven't seen a good comedy since Maeve's play about a monkey butler in Victorian society."

"I hope Sophie appreciates the lengths I'm willing to go for her," I said. "Mike seems like a real piece of work." Even worse than Lars, if that was possible.

"Please invite him back here afterward," Gareth begged.

"Not a chance," I said.

"He looks like he's ready to unbutton his pants right now," Gareth said. "Are you getting a reputation already?"

I straightened my shoulders, indignant. "Absolutely not. I've had exactly two kisses in the entire time I've been here and they were both with the same vampire."

Gareth studied me. "Was there tongue?"

I shook my finger at him. "You have no idea how much I want you to be solid right now."

Gareth chortled. "Have a good time, love. Don't be out past curfew or I'll send Sedgwick to fetch you."

Forget it, Sedgwick said from his nearby perch. *It's my night off.*

"Owls get a night off?" I queried.

It would behoove you to read the town regulations once in a while, Sedgwick said. *All messenger owls get time off.*

"But you're more than my messenger owl," I countered. "You're my familiar. I think that changes the nature of the relationship."

Sedgwick groaned. *Lawyers*, he muttered.

With a quick spritz of perfume, I rejoined Mike down-stairs and off we went.

I assumed because the date took place during dinner hours that we would actually be going out to eat dinner. My mistake. Mike drove us in his orange jalopy to the south-eastern end of town where the Shamrock Casino was located. The building had enough fey lanterns to light up New York City. The parking lot was jammed and I wondered who all these people were inside.

"I hope you're feeling lucky tonight," Mike said, giving me an obnoxious wink. "Because I sure am."

I stifled a groan. "I've never gambled before." But I was too hungry to think about gambling. They served food in a casino, right?

Together, we walked to the entrance of the casino. Mike opened the door and walked in ahead of me, not even holding the door open long enough for me to slip in behind him. Instead, the door whacked me on the back on my way in. Okay, so manners weren't his strong suit.

Blinking lights drew my attention the moment I stepped into the lobby. The interior was bright, colorful, and noisy. It reminded me of a children's arcade, except everyone in here looked well past their prime.

"Where would you like to start?" Mike asked.

I felt overwhelmed. Everywhere I turned, there were loud machines, card tables, and bodies. This was the kind of envi-ronment that triggered my anxiety.

"Why don't we start with something you enjoy?" I suggested. "If I watch for a little while, I may be able to learn a thing or two."

Mike seemed pleased by that suggestion. "Let's stop by the bar first and load up on drinks."

Load up? My stomach rumbled. I hoped appetizers were

an option. There was no way I could drink alcohol on an empty stomach, not with my track record.

The bar was located not far from the entrance to the left of the casino floor. The bar top was lower then usual and I quickly realized why. There were three bartenders working the bar right now—all leprechauns. They were, in all seriousness, absolutely adorable. I resisted the urge to pat each one on the head. Too condescending. They wore green vests trimmed in gold with black trousers. The only thing missing was a top hat. I assumed that the outfit was for the benefit of the casino rather than the way leprechauns normally dressed in Spellbound.

Mike stepped up to the bar and rapped his knuckles on the counter. "What do we need to do to get some service around here?"

Wow. We literally just arrived and Mike was acting like we'd been here for an hour. Impatience seemed to be one of his many flaws.

"Welcome to Shamrock Casino," the bartender said. He sported red facial hair and mischievous green eyes. "What can I get for you this evening?"

"I'll have an Irish special," Mike said.

The bartender's gaze shifted to me. "And for the lady?"

Mike seemed to forget I was even there. He moved aside so that I could approach the bar.

"I'm not familiar with the drinks here," I said. "What do you recommend? Anything that's light on alcohol?"

Mike elbowed me in the ribs. It was meant to be a playful gesture, but he jabbed me hard enough that I winced.

"Sorry," Mike mumbled.

"I'll have a lime tonic, please," I said. Lime tonic contained zero alcohol, which was probably for the best. "Do you have any snacks?"

Mike cast me a sidelong glance. "I thought chicks didn't eat on dates."

Chicks? "They do when they're hungry."

The leprechaun grinned at me. "I can get you some light refreshments. Tell me where you'll be playing and I'll send it over."

"We'll be at card station number four," Mike said. He turned to me. "Let's go. We're losing precious minutes."

He steered me to a card table at the far end of the casino. The table was full of players with only one seat available. Mike took it and I had no choice but to stand behind him. The woman behind the man.

"Watch and learn," he said.

It was crystal clear to me why Mike was having a hard time making a love connection. He needed someone to show him the error of his ways. Somehow, I didn't think he would welcome constructive criticism.

He set down his ale on the table and I decided to make my move. I fished the packet of powder from my pocket.

"That's a nice watch, Mike," I said. Distraction 101. "Is it real gold?"

He twisted to his left to show me the watch and I used my right hand to empty the powder into his drink. It dissolved instantly, just as Sophie promised.

"A birthday present to myself. Guess how much?"

I still didn't fully understand Spellbound money. There were a lot of gold coins and bartering. Sort of like medieval times, or what I imagined medieval times were like.

"Um, a bag of gold coins?" I ventured.

"Fifty thousand gold coins," he said, shoving the watch in my face. "It's solid, baby."

I was beginning to regret the truth powder. If Mike was this much of a braggart without magical help, I had the sinking feeling that I was about to unleash an ego monster on an unsuspecting casino.

Mike turned back to the table as the cards were dealt. The deck of cards was similar to the one Agnes had in the care home. These cards included numbers, though. They played with green and gold chips and I realized that the entire theme of the casino revolved around leprechaun lore. The flashing lights reflected the colors of the rainbow, the gold coins represented a pot of gold, and the shamrock design was on every machine. It was like an indoor theme park for Irish gamblers.

The dealer was also a leprechaun. His red beard was fully formed and he looked slightly older than the bartender. He dealt a hand to each of the seven participants. Mike was sandwiched between an elderly gnome with the requisite pointy white beard and a centaur in a derby hat. The rest of the players looked too human to identify.

Mike took a long swig of his drink and tensed when he checked his hand. It didn't take a genius to figure out that he was unhappy with it.

"That's a pretty girl you have on your arm," the elderly gnome said to Mike. "Maybe you should be a gentleman and find her a seat."

Mike kept his gaze fixed on the cards in his hand. "She knows where the chairs are."

The centaur overheard the exchange and leaned his head over. "Buddy, I'm not going to tell you how to live your life, but if you have any hope of making a good impression tonight, you might want to think twice before leaving your date on her feet behind you."

"What's the difference?" Mike said. "I'll have her off her feet later, if you know what I mean."

Bile rose in my throat, burning my esophagus. Was the powder taking effect? It was hard to tell.

"Listen, weasel," the centaur said. "I think you're being disrespectful."

Mike stuck his nose in the centaur's face. "And I think you're an abomination. So let's agree to disagree."

Oh no. I had to get Mike away from here before a fight broke out. The centaur could knock him unconscious easily. I couldn't risk missing my chance to interrogate him about Sophie.

"You know what?" I interjected. "I'd love to try a slot machine, if that's okay. I find card games slow and a little boring."

Mike tossed down the cards. "My hand sucked anyway."

The centaur shot me a sympathetic look as we left the table. It was nice to know there were gentlemen in Spellbound.

We settled in front of a slot machine. Mike never once offered me coins to play or a chance to pull the handle. It was silly of me to care, but I couldn't help it. My grandparents had instilled manners in me and that was one of the traits I had no intention of losing.

"I wore my best cologne tonight," Mike said, yanking on the handle. "It's good, right?" He bent his neck toward me and I pretended to sniff.

"Very nice," I lied. I had to speak up now. I couldn't tolerate another minute of Mike. "So I heard you're the one who spoke with the sheriff about seeing Sophie and Freddie together." I tried to keep my tone casual.

Mike was intent on the symbols flashing in front of him. "Yeah. What about it?"

"Sophie swears she was never with him," I said. "She barely knew him. We're such good friends. It hurts my feelings that she would lie to me."

Mike pulled the handle again and a few coins dropped out of the bottom. He scooped them up and continued to play. "Your friend is a tease. She acts all sweet and nice, but it's minotaur shit."

"I don't think that's true," I said. "In fact, I used a truth spell on Sophie." A necessary lie. "According to the spell, she's being honest." I waited a beat. "Which means that you aren't."

Mike's hand dropped to his side and he faced me. "She's a witch," he said heatedly. "You don't think she can get around a truth spell? Why do you think you don't use it in court? It's unreliable."

It wasn't unreliable right now.

"Newsflash Mike. Sophie is a remedial witch like me. Do you understand what that means? It means we suck at spells." At least we suck enough not to graduate from the academy and become full-fledged members of the coven. Yet.

Mike burped, not even attempting to cover his mouth. He was gross, plain and simple. "Fine. You want the truth?"

Oh, I sure did.

"I never saw Sophie with Freddie. I made it up. Happy now?" He returned his attention to the slot machine.

I stood there fuming. "Why would you lie about something so serious? Don't you understand that Sophie could go on trial because you provided false evidence?"

"Don't get all lawyerly on me," he snapped. "She ticked me off. Do you know how many times I tried to ask her out? And do you know how many times she acted like she didn't hear me or walked away before I could get the words out?" He stopped playing for a moment, reliving the experience. "She thinks she's better than me because she's a witch. Well, who's going to want her in prison?"

I shook my head in disbelief. He was willing to let an innocent young woman go to jail because she bruised his ego? Unbelievable.

"I don't know why I bother dating at all," Mike continued. "There's nothing a girl can offer me that I can't do better myself. I do a good job of taking care of my needs, if you know what I mean."

"Mike," I said, struggling to control my temper. "Your vocabulary isn't that impressive. Everyone knows what you mean." His obnoxious behavior didn't matter. I finally had what I came for. A confession. Now I could end this date once and for all.

"Emma?"

Oh no. Not now.

Slowly, I turned around. "Hi Daniel. What brings you here?"

He glanced from me to Mike, whose sole focus was still the shamrocks scrolling before his eyes.

"I came to speak with the head of marketing about contributing to a fundraiser," he said. "What are you doing here?"

Mike craned his neck. "She's on a date. Can't you see that? Hottest girl in the casino and she's with me. How do you like them burstberries?"

I shrugged helplessly at Daniel, who looked perplexed. The angel moved closer to me.

"Listen, I'm not a fan of Demetrius, you know that. But this guy is not an acceptable alternative."

There'd be time for an explanation later. Right now, I was desperate to leave.

"I'm glad you're here, Daniel," I said. "Would you mind taking home the hottest girl in the casino? My date is officially over."

CHAPTER 7

"I'm almost afraid to ask what you intend to do here," Gareth said. He surveyed the kitchen where I'd set out all of my ingredients in preparation for Operation Brownies.

"Begonia and Millie were kind enough to drop off the ingredients I need to make brownies," I said. I squinted, trying to read the instructions on the paper. I hadn't realized how difficult it was to read the handwriting.

Gareth covered his mouth in an effort not to laugh. "You're attempting to bake brownies? Why did they not stay to help?"

Magpie ran into the room and threaded his way between my legs. "Gareth, control your cat. I need to focus."

"You're far too hard on him," Gareth accused. "You're so kind to everyone else, but you treat Magpie like the toothless vampire." In solidarity, Magpie ran over and sprawled out in front of Gareth's feet.

"He smelled food," I said. "He's not in here to be nice."

"Well, you do intend to give him a nibble, don't you?"

I glared at my roommate. "He's a cat," I said heatedly. "And even that fact is debatable."

Magpie hissed at me. It was alarming how well this cat seemed to understand English.

Gareth attempted to comfort the hairless beast. "Every living thing deserves love."

It was hard to argue with that. "Have you always had an affinity for cats? Like when you were still human?" I asked as I measured out the first ingredient.

Gareth sucked in a breath—except not really because he was a vampire ghost and didn't need to breathe. "Aye, I suppose I did. Back in Scotland, I had a black-and-white cat called Haggis. He followed me everywhere—bit of a nuisance, really. My family couldn't bear him." His expression adopted a faraway quality. "I haven't thought about that in many a year. Do you think Haggis is the reason I'm so attached to Magpie?"

"I couldn't say for sure. Only you could answer that, but I think it's probably not a coincidence." I measured out the requisite amount of chocolate and began melting it in the pan. "Do you remember much of your human life? It must've been so long ago."

Gareth floated around the room, his face contorted in concentration. "Do you know what? I rarely think about it. Being a vampire just sort of takes over, you know?"

No, I didn't know, nor did I want to, but I was interested to hear about Gareth's human experience.

"Don't you guys ever reminisce about being human?" I asked. "When you socialized at the country club or at poker night, didn't you ever share your histories?"

Gareth chuckled. "No, we mostly got pissed and competed to see who had the biggest..." He smiled, showing his alabaster fangs. "Never mind."

"So you don't know how any of your vampire friends were turned?" It suddenly occurred to me that I didn't even know Gareth's story. "Is your sire here in Spellbound?" Was sire the right term for the vampire that turned him? Before Spellbound, my knowledge of vampires was limited to *Buffy* and *Twilight*.

"No, he's not here," he said. "I came to America not long after my change in circumstances. It was too difficult being around my family. They didn't want to know me anymore."

Understanding dawned on me. I glanced at Magpie and then at Gareth. "And you had to leave your cat behind." It must've been heartbreaking for him. His whole life upended in a single moment. I kneeled down and attempted to pet Magpie. He hissed and backed away, drawing closer to Gareth.

"I never really made the connection before," Gareth admitted.

"Did you leave behind anyone special?" I asked. Since Gareth was a grown man when he became a vampire, it stood to reason that he'd been in a relationship.

"No," he said. "Just family. I'd avoided attachments, but I never stopped to consider the reason why."

"Took you long enough to figure that one out."

He peered over my shoulder as I poured the chocolate from the warm pan into the mixing bowl. "What are all these other ingredients you have? Seems a bit excessive for brownies."

"Begonia says it's her family recipe. It includes some ingredients passed down within the coven."

Gareth raised a curious eyebrow. "Is that so?" He fell silent and continued to watch me work. "Are you sure you want to use so much of that yellow powder?"

I looked at the measuring cup. The powder reached the appropriate line according to the instructions. "Stop acting like a backseat driver," I snapped. "This is my baking project. You can do your own."

We both knew that wasn't true. We still hadn't figured out

whether Gareth would be able to touch anything ever again. "Have you decided whether to contact one of the Grey sisters? I'll make the arrangements. Just say the word."

Gareth became fascinated by the contents of the mixing bowl. "Not yet. But I will."

"I thought you wanted to be able to move things." Knowing Gareth, he'd take great joy in acting as a poltergeist in the house. "Why are you not making more of an effort?" It didn't make sense to me. As the public defender before me, I knew he was far from lazy. I couldn't understand his reluctance.

"What if I can't?" Gareth blurted. "What if I want to, but I can't do it?"

I stopped stirring and shook my head, baffled. "Are you seriously worried about failing?" I couldn't believe what a type A he was. "Gareth, you harass me on a daily basis about my fears and anxieties. You have no business acting afraid of failure." I meant every word. He was already a ghost. He had nothing to lose.

Gareth tried to touch the mixing bowl, but his hand simply disappeared right through it. "Fine, you've convinced me, if only to save you from attempting to bake again. While you're out dating half the town, I'll do a little investigating of my own."

I stopped mixing again to glare at him. "I am not dating half the town and you know it. I'm investigating a crime so that one of my best friends doesn't take the fall for it."

"Are you certain it has nothing to do with a certain unattainable angel?" He hesitated. "Maybe you're throwing yourself out there as a distraction?"

I set the wooden spoon on the counter and steadied myself. "Absolutely not. Daniel has nothing to do with it."

Gareth gestured toward the pan as I poured the contents of the mixing bowl into it. "You might want to go lighter on the yellow stuff next time. It's giving it a golden sheen. What did you say it was again?"

I consulted the recipe. "I'm not sure. I can't remember what the girls said it was called. They just told me to measure half a cup." I left the instructions on the counter and popped the pan into the oven. "Twenty minutes and they'll be ready for harp therapy class."

Gareth balked. "You're going to subject the members of your harp therapy class to your first attempt at baking?"

"Why do you assume that it will taste terrible? How hard is it to mess up brownies?" Oops. I probably tempted fate with that question.

"Oh, I'm sure they'll taste fine. That's not quite what I'm worried about."

My brow wrinkled. "Then what are you worried about?"

Gareth suppressed a smile. "Nothing. Nothing at all. Do carry on."

I ignored his mysterious behavior. I was sure he was just annoyed that I didn't want to follow his suggestions.

"Keep an eye on the oven for me, will you? I'm going to run up and get changed for class. Everyone's going to go crazy when they taste my brownies."

As I hurried upstairs, I heard Gareth murmur, "You can bet on it."

I showed up at harp therapy, proudly displaying my tray of brownies. I hoped my homemade brownies were as popular as the chocolate and sunshine cookies.

I noticed a few of the shifters sniffing the air as I placed the tray on the snack table.

"Ooh, brownies," Phoebe said. Phoebe Minor was Darcy's aunt and not a harpy to be trifled with. Her tongue was as sharp as her talons.

"It's my first attempt," I said, "so go easy on me."

"Don't worry, dear," she said. "It's almost impossible to mess up brownies." She shot me a pointed look. "Almost."

I watched closely as she inhaled a square. Crumbs fell from her lips and she even tried to catch them in the palm of her hand. That harpy was not letting any bit of brownie go to waste. A good sign.

"So what's the verdict?" I asked.

"Surprisingly delicious," she said. As she reached for a second square, more hands appeared. It seemed everyone in the room was now alerted to the presence of brownies.

"You made these, Emma?" Sheena asked. Sheena was a troll and the sister of Wayne, the accountant who sat on the town council.

I flashed a proud smile. "All by myself." I failed to mention Gareth's constant supervision. It seemed unnecessary. And annoying. Definitely annoying.

The brownies disappeared in a matter of minutes. I knew I should have brought a second tray. The church bell rang, alerting the attendees it was time to sit with their harps.

I took my seat between Phoebe and Sheena. Phoebe began to strum the harp strings, listening intently to the resulting sound.

"I really am quite good, aren't I?" she said.

"Not as good as me," the troll shot back. She began strumming more forcefully, as if to prove her point. These two always seemed to be in competition.

"Do you like my new haircut?" Marilee asked. The Amazon moved to stand in front of the group and swung her hair from side to side. "I think it looks amazing. Makes my neck look at least an inch more slender."

"You'll definitely get laid now," Phoebe said, nodding her approval.

My gaze flickered back to the tall girl, prepared to see an

embarrassed blush on her cheeks. Instead, she smiled broadly. "My thoughts exactly," she said.

My radar pinged. This did not strike me as normal behavior for Marilee. She tended to be the quietest person in the room.

Oslo ambled over to me. The dwarf became a fan of mine ever since I helped him gain access to the popular chocolate and sunshine cookies.

"You look pretty tonight, Emma," he said. "I was thinking that I look good tonight, too. "

I squinted at him. "Yes, Oslo," I said with uncertainty. "You do look good." What was going on?

Maeve took center stage, and began singing at the top of her voice. At the end of the verse, she threw out her hands, ready to embrace the applause.

"I really am fabulous, aren't I?" She took a bow as though she were performing on stage in her playhouse.

The group gave her a standing ovation.

Whatever was happening, I seemed to be the only one unaffected. An uncomfortable thought gnawed at me. I glanced over my shoulder at the empty tray of brownies. Could it be? But these were regular brownies. I made them myself. I didn't use any magic. I used flour, chocolate, some yellow powder...

Uh oh.

The evening carried on much the same, with each person in attendance displaying a heightened level of confidence. Marilee demonstrated her flexibility by performing various feats of yoga. I noticed the eyes of the men pinned on her as she hooked her legs behind her neck. I buried my face in my hands. Why did everything I touch turn to chaos?

"What's your problem?" Phoebe asked, nudging me in the ribs with her elbow. "Everyone's having a great time tonight except for you. Maybe you need to get yourself a haircut and a little action."

"I've had more than enough offers for action lately," I said. "Tell me, Phoebe. What do you think is your best quality?" I needed to test my theory, not that Phoebe Minor was ever hesitant to speak her mind.

"It's obviously my witty personality," she said, straight-faced.

I choked on my response. "I'm sorry. Did you say that you think your *personality* is your best quality?"

"Sure. Ask anybody."

What on earth was in those brownies? I thought it might be a dash of confidence, but maybe it was a dollop of delusion.

I turned toward Sheena. "What's your best quality?" I asked.

She leaned toward me and whispered, "I may look like a troll, but I'm a werewolf in the sack." She puffed out her ample chest with pride.

Oh boy. How long would it take for the magic to wear off? Class was only an hour long. I couldn't send the residents into town like this.

I watched in horror as Oslo asked the bendable Amazon to go for a drink after class. Talk about polar opposites. To my utter shock, she agreed. I don't know how I heard a word, though, because the sounds of the harps around me were deafening. It seemed they all believed that they were the best players in the group and were desperate to prove it tonight.

The minutes ticked by and I prayed that no one made an absolute fool of herself before the potency of the brownies faded.

"I think when I leave here, I'm going to get a tattoo," Sheena announced. "I've always wanted one, but I didn't think I could pull it off."

"Screw that," Phoebe said. "You're a troll. You can pull off anything. Tell you what, I'll go with you."

"Where do you want to go?" Sheena asked. "The Ink Stain or the Needle Gnome?"

Phoebe licked her lips. "The Ink Stain's tattoo artist is an incubus. I vote we go there."

I had to keep them from getting tattoos. If they regretted it later, it would be my head on a platter. And with a harpy involved, I had no doubt it would be my literal head on a literal platter.

"You both have such beautiful skin," I said. "Do you really want to ruin it with a tattoo?"

"What are you, my mother?" Phoebe snapped. "Do you know how many times I've had to listen to that old bag tell me what to wear and how to look to attract a man? As if I needed her help. Her cootchie has been untouched for so long, it has cobwebs."

I grimaced. "I was hoping we could all go for a drink after class." Of course, I hoped for no such thing, but I was desperate to keep them from making a permanent decision.

"You should get a tattoo with us," Sheena said excitedly. "I'm going to get the face of a wolf on my left cheek."

"Sheena," I implored. "Don't do that. Your face is so pretty."

Sheena laughed. "Not that cheek, silly."

"I want a big tongue with a piercing right here," Phoebe said, patting her hip flexor.

"I'd rather not get a tattoo," I insisted. "But I would love to spend a little time with the two of you after class. Maybe we could just go to the Horned Owl for an hour." Or two, depending on how long it took the magic to wear off.

The church bell clanged and I was filled with a mixture of relief and anxiety. Most people would be going home for the evening, so I imagined the spell would fade before they managed to get into any trouble. Phoebe and Sheena, however, were another story.

"Yes," Phoebe said. "Let's hit up the pub. Shots are on me."

"I used to love to dance on the bar there in my younger days," Sheena said.

"You're still young at heart," Phoebe said. "You get your butt up there. I want to see you shaking it in front of that bartender's face."

What had I done? As much as I wanted to get to the bottom of this, I had to see Phoebe and Sheena through the rest of the evening first.

Everyone filed out of the church and I made sure to stick close to the harpy and the troll.

Phoebe draped a wrinkled arm around me and smiled. "Hold onto your broomstick, Hart. It's going to be a bumpy night."

CHAPTER 8

My heart sank when I saw that the Horned Owl was teeming with customers. More witnesses for whatever shenanigans Phoebe and Sheena engaged in.

Phoebe pushed her way through the crowd. "Make way," she called. "Hormonal harpy coming through. If you're looking for a good time, come and sit next to me."

Sheena hobbled beside her, her broad frame bumping patrons left and right. At least these two weren't bickering. Small mercies.

Phoebe fought her way to the bar and slapped a hand on the counter. "Barkeep, three shots of Lizard Lips."

I recognized the satyr behind the bar from previous visits. Ty, one of Sophie's crushes. I caught the look of fear in his eyes when he realized one of the fiercest creatures in town was in front of him.

"Say please," Sheena admonished her. "You catch more flies with honey."

"I don't want to catch flies," Phoebe said. "I want three shots."

Behind the bar, Ty fumbled with the shot glasses.

Phoebe's presence clearly unnerved him. He poured the green liquid, careful to avoid eye contact. It was a far cry from his usual flirtation.

"How much?" Phoebe demanded.

"No charge for you, Miss Minor," Ty mumbled and moved on to the next thirsty patron.

Phoebe handed a glass to me. "Drink up, Witchy Wonder. You're only young once."

"After you," I said.

Phoebe and Sheena tossed back their Lizard Lips and slammed their glasses on the counter. Sheena wiped her mouth with the back of her hand. A classy gesture.

"Come on, Hart," Phoebe urged.

I brought the glass to my lips and blocked the stench. I had a feeling this was going to be one potent shot of alcohol.

Before I had time to react, Phoebe tipped up the bottom end of my glass and the liquid poured down my throat. It wouldn't surprise me to learn that Phoebe was forced to eat all her vegetables as a child.

Phoebe clapped her hands and let out a harpy screech. Nearly every patron in the pub winced at the unpleasant sound. Phoebe reached across the counter and grabbed Ty by the scruff of the neck.

"Turn up the music," she ordered.

Somehow, the volume increased before she released him. He immediately poured another round of shots.

"I was the most liked person in my family until Calliope came along," Phoebe said, her arm slung over my shoulders. "I bet you didn't know that."

"No, I didn't." Calliope was Phoebe's niece and widely referred to as the 'normal one.' I secretly referred to her as the Marilyn of the Munster family.

Phoebe thrust another glass into my hand. "We're going to rule this place tonight. Everyone's afraid of me." She raised her arms and turned to face the crowd. "How do you like me now, witches?"

Sheena lifted her glass in the air, but she was so short that it only went as high as my ear. "I can drink anybody here under the table. Who wants to challenge me?"

She finished the shot and began to move to the beat of the music. Phoebe grabbed her by the hand and the two older women busted out a few graphic moves I'd never seen—nor did I ever wish to see again.

When they weren't paying attention, I handed my shot to the guy next to me. He gobbled it down and gave me back the empty glass before my escorts noticed.

Black wings emerged from Phoebe's back and people shoved each other out of the way to avoid getting whacked in the face. She looped her arms underneath Sheena's armpits and flapped her wings, drifting to the top of the bar. I averted my gaze as they continued their crude dance moves on the makeshift dance floor.

"It's nice to see mature women with that kind of confidence," the man beside me said. "Very sexy."

I smiled at the older man. He looked human, but my gold coin was on shifter. "As long as they're enjoying themselves, that's what's important."

"Indeed." He shimmied his way closer to the bar. "If I can climb onto that stool without breaking a hip, I may just join them."

"Wreaking havoc again?" a familiar voice asked.

Demetrius Hunt stood beside me, looking as hot as ever in a form-fitting black T-shirt and snug jeans. Although the sexy vampire made it clear he wanted to date me, I'd decided to put the brakes on any romantic relationships while I figured out my new life—and my feelings for Daniel.

"Trying to minimize the fallout," I said.

He flashed his fangs and I fought the urge to swoon. "I'd

like to see you up there with them." He winked. "I bet you have moves I haven't seen."

"Not tonight, Dem," I said. "I have no desire to be within bump and grind distance of these two."

The vampire laughed. "How are you settling in? I heard you were spotted at speed dating on Thursday night." He cocked an eyebrow and I knew what he was really asking. Why was I actively dating when I told him I didn't want to pursue a relationship right now?

"It's not what you think," I said.

"I figured as much, especially with the options you were offered." He bumped me with his broad shoulder. "A wereweasel, really?"

"I swear to you, Demetrius. There's nowhere I'd rather be than at home in bed with a book." Any book.

He flashed those tempting fangs again. "I like the first half of that statement. Are you sure about the book, though?"

My body pulsed with energy. Why did he have to be so alluring?

"Ouch. My back," Sheena cried.

Thank the stars. Saved by a geriatric injury.

I dared to look up. Sheena was hunched over, her troll body stuck in an awkward position.

"Killjoy," Phoebe spat. "I can't ever have a night of fun with you."

"Oh, come on," Sheena said, still hunched. "It's been more fun than I've had in ages."

Phoebe cackled. "Same here." She wrapped her arms around the troll's waist and extended her wings. "I'll fly you home before you do any permanent damage."

"That's my cue to leave," I said to Demetrius. With Phoebe and Sheena out of commission, I had one more stop to make before I could head home.

. . .

I couldn't wait until morning to figure out what went wrong with the brownies. Since I already knew the identities of my prime suspects, I drove Sigmund north of town to the remedial witch hideout. The hillside hideout was a secret place for my classmates to let off steam and gripe about the coven without anyone overhearing. It was a school night, so I knew the girls were there practicing spells or watching a movie.

Standing in front of the hidden door, I realized I wasn't sure how to get in because I'd never come here alone. I pressed my palms against the dirt and tried to remember the spell I'd heard the other girls use. Thanks to the craziness at the Horned Owl, my mind was drawing a blank.

I gave up and banged my fists on the hillside, shouting their names. What I wouldn't give for a phone right now. When that failed, I resorted to the old-fashioned method of picking up a stone and chucking it at the hidden door. I chose the smallest one I could find. I didn't have the best arm and I was worried the stone would bounce off the hillside and hit me in the face. That would be just my luck tonight.

Thankfully, the hidden door materialized and Begonia stood in the doorway, her wand at the ready. When she realized it was me, she pulled me inside.

"Emma, what are you doing?"

"I need to talk to you."

Sophie and Millie sat in front of the oversized magic mirror that doubled as a movie screen, one of the secret connections to the human world. Laurel was at home, too young to be out this late on a school night.

I stopped and stared at the screen, recognizing the youthful faces of Harry, Ron, and Hermione.

"You're watching Harry Potter without me?" I began to pout but then quickly shook my head, remembering why I was there. "Please tell me what was in the brownies."

Begonia's eyes lit up. "Why? What happened?"

"I knew it," I said, pointing an accusatory finger. "My entire harp therapy class ingested those brownies. It was the weirdest class ever. The things I saw..." I squeezed my eyes closed. "I cannot un-see them. Ever."

Begonia covered her mouth. "Why did you bring them to harp therapy? We thought they were for you."

Sensing a good story, the other girls paused the movie and gave me their full attention.

"Wait," Millie said. "Your harp therapy class ate the brownies? Isn't Phoebe Minor in that group?"

I held my hands over my ears. "Please. I've heard her name quite enough for one night. Did you know she was crowned Miss Spellbound back in days of yore?" It seemed impossible that the harpy with the leathery skin and abrasive personality could have been crowned with anything other than thorns.

The other girls laughed, enjoying my distress.

"Seriously," I said, my hands moving to my hips. "What did you expect to happen to me when I ate the brownies?"

"We decided that it might help if we boosted your confidence," Sophie admitted.

Boom. A confidence enhancement. Just as I suspected. "Help what? What do I need confidence for?" While I wasn't the best student in the academy, I was making progress and my job wasn't too overwhelming right now.

Three sets of eyes took a sudden interest in the braided rug beneath their feet.

Begonia cleared her throat. "We were hoping you might tell Daniel how you really feel."

I slapped my forehead. "Are you out of your minds?"

"No, but you are," Millie said. "In the history of Spellbound, no one's managed to get as close to the Halo Hottie as you have."

"You two have a genuine connection," Begonia added. "Just like Claude and I do." A soft sigh escaped her lips.

"A connection I don't want to destroy." I shoved my hands into my pockets in a defensive gesture. "We have a great friendship and I have no interest in ruining it."

"We're sorry," Sophie said, her eyes shining with tears. "We didn't mean to cause trouble. Do you think Lady Weatherby will find out?"

Lady Weatherby seemed to be a fly on the wall of every room in Spellbound. One of her many advanced spells.

"Probably not," I said. "The residents are used to Phoebe's outrageous behavior."

Begonia tugged on my sleeve. "What did she do?"

"I can't bring myself to relive it," I said. I shoved down the memories. I needed to bury them deep within my subconscious where they could never rear their ugly heads again. "Trust me. No one ever needs to see Phoebe Minor and Sheena making a satyr sandwich."

Sophie's eyes popped. "Not my satyr?"

I couldn't lie to Sophie. "I'm afraid so. If it's any consolation, he did not look happy about it."

"Serves him right after ignoring you," Millie said. "All of his admirers can't be busty nymphs. He's got to take the bitter with the better."

Millie did not suffer fools gladly.

"I appreciate that you wanted to help me," I said. "But please let me handle Daniel on my own. My friendship with him is really important to me and I don't want to do anything to jeopardize it. I can't explain it, but you're right— we have a strong bond...I feel like I need him in my life." Need, not want. The feeling was overpowering at times and this was from someone who'd never felt like I *needed* anyone. I didn't understand it and I wasn't willing to mess with what I didn't understand.

"We are really sorry," Sophie said. "We promise we won't interfere again."

Begonia giggled. "I really wished we'd been at the Horned Owl with you. It sounds like it was quite an evening."

I groaned. "You have no idea. On the plus side, I think Phoebe and I have formed a new friendship." And I'd much rather be on the harpy's good side. In fact, it was a relief to discover that she *had* a good side.

"Sit with us and watch the rest of Harry Potter," Begonia said.

"No, thanks. I really need a good night's sleep. I have a busy day tomorrow." Again.

"You're not going back to see Agnes, are you?" Millie asked. "Because Lady Weatherby made it very clear..."

I held up a hand. "Agnes is not on tomorrow's agenda. I swear." I failed to mention, however, that another, older witch was. If Raisa wanted to be forgotten, I wasn't going to be the one to remind everyone about her. My eye began to twitch at the thought of the isolated witch in the woods. Somehow, I didn't think she was going to be the rollicking, good time that Agnes was, but I planned to bring a bottle of Fangtastic—just in case.

CHAPTER 9

I DROVE north until all signs of the town faded away, until all I could see ahead of me were hills and to the left of me only forest. The path was just as Agnes described. I would have missed it entirely except for Sedgwick, who had insisted on accompanying me.

"I don't really need an escort," I told my familiar. I could practically hear him scowling in the air above me.

What kind of familiar would I be if I let you go alone? As ornery as he was, Sedgwick was capable of the rare act of kindness.

I turned down the path and began bouncing around in my seat. Despite the magical enhancements, these tires were not made for off-roading.

Put the car in glide, Sedgwick said.

What's glide?

Did that angel tell you nothing about how your magical car works? I heard the note of disdain in his voice. *There is a button on your dashboard. I think it's green. Hit that.*

I scanned the dashboard and saw the button in question. There was an image of a car with no wheels on it. I pressed it and waited to see what happened next. The car jerked and I felt the wheels pull upward. That quickly, the journey became smooth.

Is my car actually gliding?

Yes, you can't go any higher. It's not like riding on a broomstick, but it saves your shocks.

I'm in a hovercraft, I cried. This was so cool. How could Daniel have forgotten to tell me about this function? Too focused on the state of the universe, I guess.

The car drifted along and the trees grew closer together, arching over the path in a protective stance.

I don't think you can drive any further, Sedgwick advised. *The forest is too dense up ahead.*

I pulled to the side of the path, not that I expected anyone would come along and need to pass me. I left the car and continued along the path on foot with Sedgwick directly above me.

Would you mind flying over to the right slightly? I asked.

What's the problem? Sedgwick asked. *Would you like me two paces behind you at all times as well?*

"I just don't like things directly above my head," I said.

Unbelievable, Sedgwick said. *You're worried I'm going to poop on you. Admit it.*

I kept my gaze pinned on the path ahead of me. "Maybe," I admitted.

Newsflash. I am not an infant. I can control when and where I excrete.

I glanced up at my owl. "Excrete? That's a big word for a tiny owl."

Don't patronize me, Sedgwick said, and flew ahead in disgust.

I chuckled to myself. I had to keep myself amused because, if I focused on the forest around me, I'd run screaming back to Sigmund. The path was almost nonexistent now as twisted branches and roots shoved their way out of the ground beneath my feet. Oak trees and pine trees made way for silver birches. In fact, this area of the forest seemed to be composed entirely of silver birches.

A gust of cold wind blew right through me, nearly knocking me backward. I shivered.

I see the cottage ahead, Sedgwick said.

My heart skipped a beat. Suddenly, I got the nagging feeling that this was a very bad idea. I should have at least asked Begonia to come with me. Someone to let the world know how I died.

I focused on the trail, making sure not to trip over any raised roots or wayward tree trunks. Raisa certainly didn't make it easy to visit her. I guess she was really serious about getting away from it all.

Smoke rose from the chimney of the small cottage. So she was home. That was a relief. The last thing I wanted to do was wait for her alone in the forest. She even had a white fence, although it could hardly be described as picket. As I moved closer, I realized why the fence was white. My legs wobbled slightly.

"Sedgwick, are those what I think they are?"

Afraid so, he replied and my heart sank.

Bones. The fence was made entirely of bones.

Raisa was not going to be the congenial old hag I was hoping to meet.

I had no choice but to touch the bones in order to open the gate. The second I was through, I wiped my hands vigorously on my pants. I wasn't sure what kind of germs could possibly be lingering on old bones, but still.

Are you sure about this? Sedgwick asked. *It's not too late to turn back. She doesn't know you're here.*

At that moment, the front door of the cottage swung

open and a frail woman appeared in the doorway. "Oh, but I do."

There were so many things wrong with this moment that I didn't know where to begin. The witch could hear Sedgwick? How was that possible?

"Come in, Emma Hart. I've been expecting you."

Every inch of my body told me to run. Whatever humans were programmed with regarding fight or flight, my mind and body were in agreement. Get the hell out of there! Even so, I forced myself to follow her. If Raisa was someone with answers, then I needed to push my fears aside and talk to her.

"Sedgwick is welcome to join us," she added over her shoulder.

She even knew Sedgwick's name. Agnes was right. Raisa was clearly from a different coven. But which one?

I ducked inside the small cottage. The interior was sparse. Slabs of wood seemed to be everywhere I turned. There were a few open shelves and, of course, a bubbling cauldron in the Inglenook-style fireplace. Raisa herself was frightening to behold. She looked closer to a skeleton than a person. Her legs were like two knitting needles and her nose was long and thin. Her hair was a blend of gray and white and I noticed bald patches where hair no longer grew. Between her stringy hair and the brown spots on her skin, Raisa looked like she hadn't bathed in a year.

"So what's with the bones outside?" I asked. I decided to take the direct approach. No point in being vague with someone who seemed to know so much already.

The old crone cackled softly. "It keeps out the riffraff." She gave me a pointed look. "The fact that you've already made it this far suggests that you are not one of them."

Despite the bubbling cauldron and the smoke pouring out of the chimney, the cottage itself was damp and chilly. I suddenly wished I had brought my cardigan, no matter how uptight it allegedly made me look. I tried my best not to shiver so that Raisa didn't sense my fear.

"Would you care for a drink?" she asked. "I have a few live mice for your owl. I like to be prepared."

Thank you. Sedgwick perched on a nearby post. *That would be divine.*

You're never that polite with me, I said accusingly.

I averted my gaze while Raisa pulled the live mice out of a nearby jar. Why she was saving mice in a jar, I had no idea, nor did I want to know. Whatever coven she was in, I was glad I wasn't a member of it.

Sedgwick gulped down the two mice like they were candy.

"I understand you have come looking for answers," Raisa said. "But first let me ask you, were you sent here or have you come of your own free will?"

It felt like a trick question, for which the wrong answer would result in Raisa sucking the marrow from my bones and adding me to her fence.

"I went to see Agnes in the care home," I said, deciding honesty was the best policy. "She knew that I was looking for information on my coven, so she directed me to you." I chewed my lip thoughtfully. "So I guess, technically, that means I was sent here."

Her lips spread into a wicked smile and for the first time I noticed her teeth. They were not human teeth in any way, shape, or form. They clacked together and I realized in horror that they were made of iron. Spell's bells! What on earth did a witch do with iron teeth? The bones outside took on a whole new meaning.

"What about you, Emma? May I call you Emma?"

"Yes," I stammered. "That's fine."

"You seem cold," Raisa said. "I have just the drink for you. Warms you from the inside out."

Somehow, that idea was not comforting. I didn't want to be a rude guest and decline, however. That seemed like a worse option.

Raisa hobbled over to her cauldron and lifted the huge ladle. She took a tin cup from the shelf and poured some of the bubbling liquid inside. Although I detected no odor, I was still afraid to taste it. The liquid was orange and unappealing, like drinking carrot porridge.

"Trust me, my dear," Raisa said. "You want to drink this."

I was too afraid to say no. I brought the steaming liquid to my lips and took a tentative sip. To my surprise, it tasted like orange Hi-C, one of my favorite childhood drinks. Despite the bubbles and steam, the liquid was cool as it passed my lips and slid down my throat. Only when it hit my stomach did I feel the warmth.

"Thank you," I said. "It's nice."

"Tell me how you are getting on in Spellbound," Raisa said. Now that I was aware of her iron teeth, I heard the constant click as her mouth opened and closed. The sound was unnerving.

"It's been quite an adjustment," I admitted. "But I have met some wonderful friends and that's made a huge difference."

She gave me a sly look. "Yes. Your friends. You mean that scoundrel, the angel."

"Not just Daniel. Other witches in the academy. Lucy, the fairy who works for Mayor Knightsbridge. My roommate…" I said.

"The dead vampire," she finished for me. "How is that for you? I take it you'd never seen a ghost before. Not in the human world."

So she knew that, too. Was she reading my mind or did she have that special way of knowing things like Lady Weatherby?

"Gareth has been a welcome addition to my life," I said

truthfully. "He can be a pain sometimes, but the pros far outweigh the cons." I took another sip of the brew. "Agnes suggested that you were never the head of the coven here, but the way she said it suggested there was a story there. Care to tell me about it?" My question seemed both brave and stupid at the same time.

The bony witch studied me carefully. "Why would I be the head of a coven that wasn't mine?" She hobbled over to the wooden chair beside the fireplace and rested her frail body. "I'm sure she told you that I was alone here, the sole witch from my coven."

"How did that even happen? Were you already living here on your own? Had you separated from your coven?"

"I was only passing through Ridge Valley when the curse took hold. I had no plans to settle here. Funny that, plans have a way of changing in the blink of an eye. Seems to me you've learned that yourself."

The hard way. "So you were sort of like me? You were in the wrong place at the wrong time?" I polished off the rest of my drink and set the tin cup on a nearby butcher's block.

"We are similar in many ways," she said with an air of mystery. "How did it feel to learn that you were a witch?"

"It was a shock. I can say that much. I never had any indication that I was different."

"Tell me about your owl," she said. Her haggard face softened and I caught a glimpse of the witch she once was.

"I met Sedgwick at Paws and Claws," I began.

She flicked a dismissive finger. "Not him. Tell me about Huey."

My eyes widened. How could she possibly know about Huey?

"He was my stuffed animal when I was little. I took him everywhere with me."

"Your mother gave him to you." It was more of a statement than a question.

I nodded and felt the tears brimming in my eyes. Any mention of my mother brought the threat of tears. "It was the last present she gave me before she died."

"She drowned," Raisa said. "A tragic ending for a witch. It is the worst kind of death."

Gee, thanks for that. I always wanted to imagine my mother dying in agony.

"I don't know whether she knew she was a witch," I said. "I don't have any memories that suggest she knew. And my father certainly never mentioned anything."

"Humans have a funny way of dealing with things they don't understand. Denial, suppression, lashing out." She shook her head. "It was inevitable that you would end up here."

Inevitable?

"Did you know that your owl can see and hear your vampire ghost?"

I shot a suspicious look in Sedgwick's direction. "Are you sure?" I was certain that I was the only one who could communicate with Gareth.

Raisa smiled. "He is your familiar. He has a strong connection to you and that includes absorbing some of your abilities."

"Were you planning to keep this a secret forever?" I asked Sedgwick.

The owl turned his head one hundred and eighty degrees away from me. *The less competent you think I am, the less you will ask me to do.*

As annoyed as I wanted to be, I understood his logic. When I was younger, I used to pretend that I was terrible at dusting so that I didn't have to do it. I would deliberately leave layers of dust on tabletops so that my grandmother wouldn't assign me that particular chore. I could load a dishwasher like nobody's business, but I hated dusting. I was so grateful for Fiona's fairy cleaning service. The Magic Touch made my life much easier, especially given Gareth's old house. It attracted cobwebs like Daniel attracted women.

"We'll have to share this news with Gareth," I said. "It wouldn't be fair to keep it from him." Especially when they were home alone so often. Who knew what Gareth got up to when I wasn't there? He'd be embarrassed to learn that Sedgwick had witnessed it all.

"What about his cat?" I asked. Magpie wasn't anyone's familiar, but he didn't strike me as an ordinary cat.

Raisa licked her lips. "The cat's connection to the vampire is strong enough to pierce the veil. Vampires don't have familiars, but the cat is as close as he could possibly get to one."

"So which coven are you a member of?" I asked.

"None," she said. "I'd already been shunned when I arrived here. Sometimes separation is for the best."

"Agnes seemed to think you might be able to tell me something about my coven," I said. "So far, I can communicate with Gareth and I have an owl as my familiar. Those seem to be the biggest differences between the witches here and me. Oh, and I'm pretty handy with the non-rhyming spells."

Raisa nodded sagely. "There will be more. As time unfolds, you will discover them." Her gaze drifted to my feet. "You also prefer your feet on the ground. Not necessarily the trait of a witch."

Was she speaking metaphorically? Or was she referring to my fear of heights?

"Do you think my anxiety is connected to my coven?" It seemed unlikely. The idea of an entire coven of anxious witches seemed more like the premise of a half-hour comedy.

"I could not say for certain," she said. "And what of your birthmark? Have you ever considered that it could be a clue?"

Birthmark? "I don't have a birthmark."

She smiled and heaved a sigh. "Something else for you to discover then. I'll leave that to you."

"Why do you want to be forgotten?" I asked. I wasn't sure what made me ask the question. Part of me was afraid she'd use those iron teeth to tear my flesh from my limbs in response.

"I'm not like you, Emma Hart. I never wanted to belong to anyone or anything. Solitude suits me."

"I don't mind being alone," I said. I'd spent my adult years alone until now. Granted, having so many nice people around me in Spellbound was a welcome change.

"I think you know what I mean," Raisa said. She hauled herself to her delicate feet. "I believe your time is up. I have enjoyed our conversation. It's been so long since I had a visitor."

"Before I go," I said, "I know there are other people in town who can communicate with ghosts." Like Maeve McCullen. "What about seers? Is there anyone here who can see the future?"

"No one here can tell you the answers you seek, my dear," she replied. "There is one seer in town who may be able to offer you some guidance, however limited. Her name is Kassandra. Spelled with a K." She rolled her eyes and I strangled a scream when one of her eyeballs popped out of the socket.

Cool as a cucumber, she scooped the eyeball off the floor and stuck it back in place.

"Thank you, Raisa," I stammered. "I appreciate you taking the time to speak to me." I glanced at the empty tin cup. "Just out of curiosity, what was the brew?" I half expected it to be poison.

"It's called Pure of Heart," she replied with an uneven cackle.

"So it was magic?" Nothing seemed to happen.

"You passed the test," she said. "Had you not been pure of heart, you'd be dead by now. Your skin melted and a pile of bones on the floor. Fodder for my fence."

My saliva stuck in my throat. "Good to know," I squeaked. "If you ever get bored of isolation, please feel free to stop by my house. Sedgwick and I would welcome you."

Speak for yourself, he said.

"Oh, my child," she said. "Thank you."

She dragged herself to the door and opened it. "Be sure to be out of the forest by sundown. You won't want to meet the night creatures here. Trust me on that."

If the witch with iron teeth and a bone fence was telling me I didn't want to meet the night creatures, then I definitely didn't want to meet the night creatures.

Sedgwick and I left the cottage and my pace quickened once we left the yard.

Well, that was interesting, Sedgwick said, hovering above me.

I glanced upward. "To the right, please." I paused. "Are you sure interesting is the word you mean?"

He shifted to the right above me. *Okay, fine. She was terrifying.*

"Thank goodness. I was afraid it was just me."

We made it out of the forest before sundown, much to my relief. As I crossed over Hawthorne Drive, I saw a familiar cloaked figure riding a magic bicycle. I touched the window of the car and the pane of glass disappeared.

"Professor Holmes," I called.

He cast a sidelong glance at me. "Emma," he said warmly.

"Where have you come from? It's rather desolate in that direction."

"I went to see Raisa. Agnes had suggested that I go see her to ask about my coven."

"Ah, yes," he said. "The old cottage with the bones. Creepy place, isn't it?"

"She wasn't as scary as I thought she'd be," I said. Then I laughed. "Okay, who am I kidding? She was downright terrifying. I was afraid at any moment those iron teeth would go to town on me. I was wondering if I should've left a trail of breadcrumbs, but Sedgwick probably would've eaten them."

Professor Holmes gave me an odd look. "You…conversed with her?"

"Oh, I know. She likes her solitude. She didn't seem to mind an unexpected visitor. I mean, most people hate the drop in, but I guess when you're alone three hundred and sixty-four days a year, you tend to overlook manners."

Professor Holmes cleared his throat. "Emma, I hate to be the one to tell you this, but Raisa died last year."

I burst into laughter. "No, we just came from her." I glanced skyward at Sedgwick. "Didn't we?" Not that Professor Holmes could hear the owl's answer.

"She wanted to be forgotten, so in her parting letter she requested a quiet burial on the grounds of the cottage. I attended the burial personally. I'm not surprised that Agnes didn't know. She's been in the care home for many years now."

A slow chill started at the nape of my neck and crept to every fiber of my being. "But she could touch things. Move things." Her eyeball popped out!

"I shall report the matter to Lady Weatherby," he said. "You can trust our discretion." He rode off, leaving Sedgwick and I in the dust.

Well, that was unexpected, Sedgwick said.

"I'll have to break the news to Gareth," I said. "He isn't the only ghost in my life anymore." I can't say I was excited by the prospect.

If she is truly a ghost, then maybe Gareth doesn't need the help of a Grey sister after all, Sedgwick said. *Maybe we could enlist the aid of Raisa.*

Given the choice between an eyeless, toothless woman and a witch with iron teeth and a bone fence, I knew which one I'd choose.

"Hmm. I think I'll leave the decision to Gareth."

CHAPTER 10

MY MORNING WAS DEVOTED to preparing Thom's testimony for trial. Although he was clear and consistent in his responses, I wanted him to practice toning down his anger. He wasn't yelling or slamming his fist on the table. Rather, it was a quiet, simmering anger that I felt every time he spoke.

"Do I really sound angry?" Thom asked, after a third attempt at answering my practice question. "I don't hear it."

"I don't hear it either. I feel it," I said. "You have unexpressed emotions, I think, and it's coming through in your testimony."

"Well, I should be angry, right?" He crossed his arms. "I mean, I'm on trial because my ex framed me. Doesn't it make sense to be mad?"

"No one likes an angry person," I said. "It makes others uncomfortable. We don't want the judge to have a negative impression of you."

He gnawed at his fingernails. "I've been doing a lot more work lately, trying to channel my...whatever. I even made a T-Rex skeleton out of wood. How cool is that?"

I came out from behind the desk to sit beside him.

"Thom, it's perfectly okay to have feelings and express them. I think it's great that you're using carpentry to channel your emotions. It's healthy." At least that's what Lady Weatherby's psychology class taught me.

"Then why do I sound angry now?" he asked. "It must not be helping."

"You're still hurting," I said. "You're not over Lara and now you have to face her all over again because of the trial." I gave his arm a sympathetic squeeze. "Maybe when you give your answers, focus on the positive feelings you once had toward her. That might take the edge off."

He nodded, understanding. "She'll be there, won't she?"

"Yes," I said. "She'll be testifying, too."

"I don't want her to hear the hurt and anger in my voice," he said firmly. "Let's try it again."

I resumed my position behind the desk and did my best impression of the prosecuting attorney.

"Now you sound angry," Thom said, smiling.

"I was going for pompous."

He scrutinized me. "Hmm. I think you're going to have to work on that."

Thom laughed again and I felt his anger slowly dissipating. Working through emotions was more often a marathon than a sprint, but I knew he'd get there in the end. With any luck, we all would.

Although I'd left the details of Mike's confession at Sheriff Hugo's office, I decided to follow up with Astrid, his Valkyrie deputy. I wanted to make sure that the sheriff was taking the confession seriously and not still considering Sophie as a suspect.

Sedgwick flew my message to her, requesting a meeting at Perky's that morning. Although I preferred the lattes at

Brew-Ha-Ha, I was becoming familiar with the sheriff's routine and knew he was less likely to turn up in Perky's. The coffee shop was smaller and less popular than Brew-Ha-Ha, probably due to the location.

Astrid was standing at the counter when I arrived, chatting with the barista. Tall, blond, and ready to wrestle you to the ground with one hand tied behind her back, she was hard to miss.

"Got your message, Emma," Astrid said. "That owl of yours is a real charmer, you know that?"

I couldn't tell whether she was being serious. As far as I was concerned, Sedgwick's charm lay somewhere between curmudgeon and serial killer.

"I got you a cinnamon latte," she said, handing me a steaming mug. "I hope that's okay."

A plain cinnamon latte? I didn't want to seem ungrateful, but all of my Spellbound lattes to date included a shot of a magical ingredient. A cinnamon latte was so…human.

"Thank you," I said, opting for politeness. "Do you already have a table?"

Astrid nodded toward the small table in front of the window. Although I didn't necessarily want to be on display, the cobblestone sidewalk in front of Perky's wasn't exactly a main thoroughfare.

"I heard you were at the Shamrock Casino recently," Astrid said, choosing the seat that faced the room. I suspected it was the deputy inside her that didn't want her back to the room.

I blew the steam from my latte. "The gossip mill here never ceases to amaze me. Who told you?"

She laughed. "Your owl."

I scowled. My own familiar was responsible for sharing the details of my personal life? Sedgwick and I would be having a tense conversation later.

"That's sort of the reason I wanted to meet with you." I sucked the foam off the top of my drink. Always the best part. "My date was Mike."

"Our wereweasel witness? That's a coincidence."

"Not really." So Sheriff Hugo had chosen not to share the confession with his deputy. Typical. "I slipped a truth powder into his drink and he admitted that he'd made up the story about seeing Sophie with Freddie."

Astrid rolled her eyes. "What a little weasel."

"Exactly. Apparently, he was annoyed with Sophie for rejecting his advances, so he thought framing her was the ideal way to express his displeasure."

Astrid's nostrils flared. "I'll make sure Sheriff Hugo wipes his statement from the investigation. And he's lucky I don't wipe up the floor with him. If he so much as gets a parking ticket, he'll regret it."

I knew I could count on Astrid. "Thanks. I should warn you, though. I'd already given the information to Sheriff Hugo days ago."

Astrid pressed her lips together. "I see."

"Sophie is the sweetest person in Spellbound. I've hated seeing her stressed about this." And Mike was a loser who deserved to spend an hour trapped in a room with Lady Weatherby. Maybe I could arrange that...

"I'll make sure he gives the confession the attention it deserves. Don't think for one second he'll remove Sophie from the top of his suspect list, though," Astrid warned. "She's still the one he found in front of the coffin with her wand out."

"I know." And I knew how the sheriff operated. Lazy mode.

"You'll be pleased to know that the sheriff has been willing to consider other theories," Astrid said. She sipped her coffee and smiled. "If nothing else, you seem to have convinced him to up his game."

"Really?" A shred of good news.

"Well, he'd still rather golf than follow up on a lead, but he's making more of an effort. Just yesterday he went to see Pandora."

"The matchmaker?"

Astrid nodded. "It seems that Freddie was a client."

I'd completely forgotten about Pandora. Estella told me that he'd had a date thanks to the matchmaker.

"It seems Freddie was involved in speed dating and a matchmaking service," Astrid said. "Talk about desperate for a love connection."

Some people crocheted or learned to play the harp. Apparently, Freddie's hobby was looking for love.

"Why do you think he was so invested in finding a girl-friend?" I asked. He didn't strike me as particularly old.

Astrid gave me a rueful smile. "Don't we all want to find that special someone?"

"I guess." I sighed inwardly. What if I'd already found my special someone but just couldn't have him?

Astrid drained the remaining coffee from her mug. "His sister is married with kids. His father is dead and his moth-er's in the care home. He probably felt it was time to make his own family."

I understood the desire all too well. "He has friends, though. People who matter to him." Sometimes friends made the best family members.

Astrid set down her mug and chuckled. "Heidi. She's been checking in with us every day to see what's new in the inves-tigation. I think she's driving the sheriff a little nuts."

"Not a difficult thing to do," I said.

"I think she may have replaced you as the sharpest fang in

his side at the moment. Last time she dropped by, he pretended to have someone in his office."

I shrugged. "Not to worry. I'll be sure to reclaim my crown soon enough."

"We're going to get to the bottom of this soon," Astrid said. "The longer Freddie remains unconscious, the harder the spell will be to break."

I rolled up my sleeves, my jaw set. It was time to pay a visit to a matchmaker.

To be honest, I was a little embarrassed to be seen heading into Pandora's office. Although it was silly, I didn't want anyone to think I needed a matchmaker in order to meet someone. Granted, most of Spellbound knew that I'd rejected Demetrius Hunt's advances, so they knew I was capable of attracting a member of the opposite sex.

The bell jingled softly as I entered the building. The interior was not what I expected. While the chairs and coffee table were typical of an office, the style was pure luxury. The sofa was covered in crushed velvet and the chairs were soft and inviting, laden with sparkling throw pillows. The top of the coffee table was glass and the brass legs were shaped like giant leaves. The room belonged in a Las Vegas casino.

Pandora was not what I expected either. I knew she was a nymph and friendly with many of the town's more esteemed residents. She was meeting with a client when I arrived. Her office was set off from the rest of the room by a glass wall. Although I could see inside, I couldn't hear their conversation. I sat on the plush sofa and waited my turn. After about thirty minutes, the glass door finally opened and the client stepped into the room. I didn't recognize him, but his fangs made him easily identifiable. He was attractive, not as scorching hot as Demetrius, but still. I wondered why he felt the need for a matchmaker. I must've been staring at him because he flashed me a smile.

"Good day to you, Miss Hart," he said.

He knew me? Despite my celebrity claims, I was surprised that he actually was able to put a face to a name. Maybe he was friendly with Demetrius.

"Hi," I managed to squeak.

Pandora waved to me from behind her gleaming silver desk. I rose from the sofa and entered the fishbowl.

Pandora smiled at me. She was pretty in a crisp sort of way, with cropped silver hair and a flawless complexion. She wore a simple black dress and the matching suit jacket was lined with glittering gemstones.

"Emma Hart. I must admit, I never expected to see you in here. You are on every eligible bachelor's shortlist. Don't you know that?"

I felt the heat rush to my cheeks. "That's nice to know, I guess. I'm not actually here about me, though."

"That's a shame," Pandora said. "I could have you on a date every night of the week if you're interested." She gave me a coy look. "You'd never have to pay for a meal again."

Given my culinary skills, the offer was mildly appealing.

"Just out of curiosity," I said, "why would a vampire like that guy need your services?"

Pandora glanced at the now empty room. "Killian Muldoon. Such a nice guy. It's a mystery why he has trouble meeting anyone. That's why we're setting up an evaluation."

"An evaluation?" I echoed. "What does that involve?"

"I arrange a date with an enthusiastic young woman," Pandora explained. "I observe the date and get feedback from the young woman afterward. Then we present Killian with a list of suggested improvements."

"He must be hundreds of years old," I said. "Hasn't he had plenty of experience?"

"He wants to be in a relationship. Vampires like Demetrius Hunt, for example..." Her brow rose suggestively. "They're not interested in a relationship. They want the action but not the quiet moments. Killian wants it all. Generally, if a vampire wants that kind of life, he gets it. So there's obviously a disconnect between what Killian is saying and what he's doing."

"Isn't it possible that it's just intimidating for young women to know that she's in a relationship with an immortal?"

"I would agree with you," Pandora said, "except for the fact that he hasn't been able to attract a vampire mate either. He wants to spend eternity with someone and it's my job to make that happen."

Well, I guess it was nice that she took her role seriously. When you live in the same town as all of your clients, that's probably an incentive to get it right the first time.

"So if you're not here for yourself, why are you here?"

"It's my understanding that you arranged a date for Freddie. I was hoping you could tell me more about it."

Pandora chewed her lip. "I spoke to Sheriff Hugo about this already. Are you sure you want to follow in his hooves? From what I've heard, that's become your specialty."

"I'm glad to hear he's spoken with you," I said. "I was concerned that he would only focus his attention on Sophie."

Pandora smiled gently. "I must say, it cheers me that you've bonded with members of the coven. I like loyalty in a person." She blew out a regretful breath. "But I must tell you what I told the sheriff. My client files are confidential. Freddie is still alive, therefore, his file remains confidential. The same goes for the young woman he met through me. She has a right to confidentiality, too."

"You're not a medical professional or a lawyer," I said. "Why should your confidentiality agreement trump a criminal investigation?" I knew rules were different in Spell-bound, but that seemed ridiculous.

"It would destroy my business if clients believed I would hand over their personal information at the drop of a wand," she said. "Spellbound has rules to protect businesses. We don't have the luxury of upping sticks and reopening in another town."

I squinted at her. "But you just divulged to me the reason Killian was here. Isn't that confidential information that you voluntarily shared?"

Pandora gave me an approving smile. "You're smart. I like that. In truth, I was hoping you might show an interest in him. That's the only reason I told you about him. I figured perhaps Demetrius was too much of a player and you were looking for someone more…permanent."

An idea began to take shape. "What if I became your client? Would you be at liberty to share information about potential matches with me?"

"If you'll fill out this questionnaire, we can get started immediately." She slid a paper and quill across the desk.

I skimmed the disclaimers and initialed next to the fee. It wasn't as expensive as I anticipated.

"I'll give you this file on one condition." Pandora's fingers pressed down on the folder.

"What's the condition?"

"I need you to go on a date with one of my clients."

"Don't you need to arrange dates for all of your clients?" I asked. "Isn't that basically your job?"

Pandora smiled. "You don't understand. He's a long-standing client and I haven't had much luck matching him to anyone."

My skin began to crawl. Was I about to agree to go out with a hideous monster?

"What's wrong with him?"

"Absolutely nothing. That's the problem. He is intimi-dating to women and he has very high standards on top of that." She shook her head. "It makes for a very difficult client."

"If he's that picky," I said, "what makes you think he'll agree to go out with me?"

"Are you kidding me? You'd be the most hotly requested client on my roster."

It wasn't the first time I'd been told that. It made sense. When you were surrounded by the same people day in and day out for eternity, the new person was as rare as a unicorn and equally desirable.

"If your client agrees to go out with me, then it's a deal." It was a no-brainer.

"I'll send an owl his way," she said. "I'll let you know as soon as I hear from him, but I'm sure it will be a go."

"Can you tell me anything about him?"

"His name is Fabio," she said, and I nearly choked on my tongue. "He's a shifter, a werelion."

"Let me guess," I said. "He's best known for his luxurious mane."

Pandora tilted her head and squinted. "How did you know? Have you met him?"

"No, but I'm really looking forward to it."

"Excellent." Pandora rifled through the folders on her desk. "Look at this. I may have someone else of interest to you." She set a folder in front of me. "How do you feel about dwarfs?"

I smiled. "Love 'em. Tell me everything there is to know."

I sat in my office, perusing Freddie's file. It turned out he'd been on a string of dates before his coma. Remembering what Estella told me, I decided to start with his most recent date and work in reverse.

Althea entered the office with a watering can.

"Are these plants for your benefit or mine?" I asked, staring at the three plants on the windowsill.

"They were for Gareth's benefit and I got in the habit of taking care of them," she replied. She poured water into the soil and watched as it settled.

"He doesn't have plants in his house. Why have them here?"

"He spent most of his time here," she said. "I think the plants were a reminder of what it was like to be alive." She glanced quickly around the room. "He's not with you, is he?" Althea knew about Gareth's ghost, although she couldn't see him.

"No, I've been out most of the day."

"What do you suppose he does stuck in that house all day?" she asked. The hiss of her snakes drew my attention to her headscarf. I wasn't sure I'd ever get used to the presence of snakes in my office.

"Raids my underwear drawer," I said. Or he would, if he could figure out how to move objects.

Althea smiled. "Why do I get the sense that your underwear isn't girly enough for him?"

"Good point." I held up a paper in the file. "Do you know a young fairy named Cecily?"

Althea placed a hand on her ample hip. "You're asking the wrong Gorgon, girl. I don't socialize with anyone under the age of thirty."

"Why not?"

"Because at that age, they care too much what others think. By the time they're my age, they let their hair down and embrace their true selves." She winked at me. "That's much more fun to be around."

The thought of Althea letting her hair down made me shudder. All those snakes. Brrr.

"Are you chilly?" she asked. "You should keep a sweater in here. I always have a cardigan on the back of my chair."

"I'm fine, thanks." No need to say that her snakes creeped me out. That seemed rude.

"You remind me so much of Gareth," she said with a laugh and I froze.

"I remind you of Gareth?" On what planet did I remind her of a gay Scottish vampire ghost?

"You both want to be 'fine' all the time. He never wanted help either. Always had to do everything himself." She paused, remembering. "Sometimes it was hard to justify my existence here."

"I ask for help when I need it," I argued.

"Is that so?" She pressed her palms against my desk and leaned forward to inspect the file. "What's that you're reading? Freddie's dating file?"

I closed the folder. "Sophie needs my help. Sheriff Hugo will pin this on her if he can get away with it."

"One of these days the sheriff is going to cross the line," Althea said.

"One of these days?" I echoed. "I think he crosses the line every day. I can't believe the residents put up with his shoddy work. It's offensive."

Althea suppressed a smile. "Like I said, you and Gareth are like two wings on the back of a Pegasus."

"Hold down the fort," I said. "I'm going to see if I can find this fairy at the salon where she works. She may have information about Freddie."

"If you need any help," Althea called, "don't hesitate to ask. That's why I'm here, even though you both seem to forget that fact."

I missed the last part of her sentence because I was already out the door.

CHAPTER 11

ACCORDING TO THE FILE, Cecily worked at Glow. The salon was nestled in the righthand corner of the town square, next to Taffy's candy shop. I hadn't been to the salon yet. My hair tended to grow very slowly and, in the human world, I never had enough money for extras like massages or manicures.

I marveled at the interior of the salon. Enchantment was everywhere I looked. Colorful tools floated in mid-air and the whole room seemed dusted in sparkles. A pair of hot pink scissors worked their way around the edges of a gnome's hair, while a hose danced above another customer's head, ready to rinse. If the jobs were magically automated, what did a stylist do here?

A fairy fluttered toward me, a lemon yellow wand in her hand. "Welcome to Glow. Have you been here before?"

"Uh, no," I replied, still unable to focus. The ambience was overwhelming.

"I'll bet you're here for a massage," she said, offering a sympathetic smile. "You look like you need to relax."

"Well, actually…"

"I'll tell you what. Cecily had a cancellation, so she has an opening right now." She began to steer me toward the back room.

Cecily was a masseuse? Instead of resisting, I allowed the fairy to guide me to the massage alcove.

"Can I offer you a ziggleberry infusion while you're waiting?" the fairy asked. "It's wonderfully hydrating."

"No, thank you." With my kernel-sized bladder, I'd need to pee five minutes into the massage.

"Cecily will be with you in a moment." The fairy pointed to a fluffy robe. "Feel free to use the dressing room and change into the robe. Trust me, you've never worn anything so comfortable."

I waited until she left to duck into the dressing room. Was I really planning to interrogate a potential suspect while she gave me a massage? I slipped off my clothes and pulled on the robe.

The fairy was right. It was like wearing a cloud.

"Miss? Are you ready?"

Cecily hovered outside the dressing room door. She was a petite fairy with green wings and matching green eyes. Although the front of her hair was black, the part in a ponytail was bright white.

"You must be Cecily," I said. "I'm Emma."

"Happy to have you." She looked me up and down. "It's a good thing you're here. The stress is rolling off of you. The way you hold your shoulders, so rigid—do you suffer from frequent headaches?"

Her remark only served to make me more rigid. It was the equivalent of telling someone to smile. It only made the person want to frown more.

I followed Cecily down a narrow hallway to a private room and she waited outside until I discarded my robe. The massage table was so high that it was connected to a small ladder. Once I was facedown on the table, I realized why. Cecily appeared beside me, her wings fluttering rapidly.

"What kind of massage would you like today?"

I had no clue what to say. I'd never had a human massage so I had no frame of reference. "Whatever makes the most sense for a tense person."

"Perfect. I'll do the Miracle."

She gently touched the nape of my neck with her wand and the tightness faded. Miracle, indeed.

"I haven't seen you here before," Cecily said. "Where do you normally go for massage?"

"I'm new in town," I said. "I haven't been anywhere for massage in Spellbound."

I felt her stop mid-motion. "You're that new witch?"

"Emma Hart," I said. It wasn't easy to talk when your face was pressed against a cushion.

She flew around me in a frenzy, pointing her wand at each body part and uttering a magic word. My body responded to each command, the tension dwindling.

"Wow," she said. "I can't believe you're from the human world. I'm so jealous."

"Really? But everything here is so cool. And the variety of residents. Trust me, there are no fairies in Lemon Grove, Pennsylvania."

"There are," she said. "You just didn't know it."

"Your dating pool is so much more interesting than ours," I continued. "Vampires, werewolves, dwarfs…" I slightly emphasized the last word, hoping for a reaction.

"Dating a dwarf is no different than dating a vampire, in my opinion," she said. "Males are all the same."

"How so?"

I heard her huff with annoyance. "They're rude to you and then can't understand why you don't want to date them again. Like it's no big deal to disrespect me."

"I know plenty of guys like that in the human world."

"Too bad. I was hoping it would be better out there. Maybe if this curse ever lifts, I'll get to find out for myself."

"Have you had a recent bad experience?" I asked. "I've been using Pandora's matchmaking service and I'm hoping she chooses her candidates wisely."

In her excitement, Cecily slapped my butt and I flinched. "You're kidding! I'm using her, too. Can't say I've been impressed with the results so far."

"No? Why not?"

"The last guy…" She trailed off. "Forget it."

I craned my neck to look at her. "You can tell me. I'm a captive audience."

She resumed her massage work with the wand and my muscles were grateful. "I don't want to say anything negative because he's…he's the dwarf in the glass coffin."

I feigned surprise. "Your most recent date was with Freddie?"

"Do you know him?" Cecily shook her head. "I guess not, since you're new in town." She focused on my feet, which hurt more than I realized, probably because I spent weeks walking in and out of town before Daniel presented me with a magically-enhanced Sigmund.

"I don't know him," I confirmed. "So feel free to talk to me if you want. Was he a jerk?"

"Kinda," she replied. "He seemed so eager to go out with me, but once we were on the date, he acted like he had a hundred better things to do."

"Not a good listener?"

"Not a good anything," Cecily replied. "I'd say something and he'd just look at me, like the words didn't register. I'd have to repeat it."

"Maybe there was something serious going on that he didn't want to talk about and it was distracting him." I felt a knee-jerk desire to give Freddie the benefit of the doubt. So far, residents had nothing but positive things to say about him. Cecily was the first one to complain.

"Then cancel the date," she huffed. "Don't waste my valuable time. I could've gone out with someone different and met my true love that night instead of sitting across from Freddie."

Sheesh. I guess Cecily wasn't shooting for fairy godmother status anytime soon—I had to imagine empathy was a requirement.

"Well, Freddie's not wasting anyone's time now, sadly."

Cecily's wand dropped to her side. "I sound angry, don't I?"

"A little bit." Angry enough to seek revenge?

"I'm such an awful fairy." She perched on the edge of my table and I heard the sound of gentle sobbing. "No wonder he didn't like me. I only think about myself. 'Cecily Mae, you're never going to meet anyone. Not if you insist on being the topic of every conversation.' That's what my mother always says." She blinked away her tears and looked at me. "Freddie's probably in that coffin because of me. I bored him into an endless sleep."

She began to sob in earnest. I sat up and patted her on the back.

"It's not your fault, Cecily." *But good job with making Freddie's endless sleep about you*, I thought. *It takes real talent.*

"The truth is Freddie was really nice to me," she sniffed. "Very polite. He just didn't seem interested and I wondered why he chose to date me in the first place."

That part was, indeed, a mystery. By all accounts, Freddie was in the market for a serious relationship. Why would he choose someone he had no interest in? And his mother thought he was excited about his date with Cecily. Why would he pretend?

"Cecily." I bit my lip, wanting to choose my words carefully. "Did you ever get the sense that Freddie might be more interested in men?" Maybe he was going through the motions for the benefit of others, but his heart wasn't in it. Like Gareth's engagement to Alison.

Cecily shrugged. "I don't think so. He said enough to give the impression that he was into women."

"Did he compliment your outfit?" Because that wasn't necessarily a clue. Gareth had stolen Alison's sparkly pink cardigan and I'd originally thought it was for sentimental reasons rather than because he liked to wear it.

"He noticed my hairstyle." She smoothed the top of her head. "He said his best friend Heidi used to wear her hair like that."

Heidi again. "Did he talk about Heidi a lot?"

"Considering he didn't say much—yeah, I guess so."

"Did he mention Paul at all?"

She frowned. "Who's Paul?"

"Heidi's boyfriend."

Cecily took a tissue out of her shirt in order to wipe her nose and I wondered whether the tissues formed the padding of her bra. An old-school fairy.

"He didn't mention anyone named Paul."

If Heidi talked about Freddie as often as Freddie talked about Heidi...How did Paul feel about their relationship?

"Thanks for the massage, Cecily," I said. Despite the tearful interruption, I still felt ten times better than when I arrived.

"Oh, I'm so sorry," she said. "This was very unprofessional. Please don't tell anyone. I don't want to lose my job."

"I wouldn't do that," I assured her.

"I'll tell them to use my friends and family discount," she said. "I do hope you'll come back. The next miracle massage will be more...miraculous, I promise."

"You know what, Cecily? I will." And I meant it.

I almost didn't see him as I zoomed past the corner of Basil and Nutmeg Lanes. He was hard to miss, though, crammed into a tiny seat behind a table with his white wings spread wide behind him. The sign on the table read 'lemon fizz – 10 coins.' I pulled the car over and went to investigate.

"Hey, Daniel? What are you doing?"

He smiled up at me. It was rare that I found myself looking down on the tall angel.

"I'm raising money for Shifter Scouts, Pack number 413," he said proudly.

"Why? Shouldn't the scouts be selling their own lemon fizz?"

He poured a cup of the golden bubbling liquid and handed it to me. "For you, on the house."

Begrudgingly, I accepted the drink. "Daniel, I'm not trying to be a Debbie Downer, but how is selling lemon fizz making up for past transgressions?"

His gaze dropped to the pitcher in front of him. "I may have wronged a member of a shifter pack at one time. She was a single mom and both of her daughters were Shifter Scouts."

"So why not make amends with the mother? Why raise money for a troop of girls who weren't impacted by your bad behavior?"

"It was a long time ago," he explained. "They're no longer living."

Spell's bells. How far back did his bad boy routine extend? Would he be apologizing to all of the animals spawned from those that hitched a ride on Noah's ark?

"I think it's nice that you're helping," I said. "But don't you think there's a better use of your time?"

121

He spread his arms wide. "I have nothing but time. Tomorrow I'm chaperoning the high school dance because one of the teachers is out sick this week."

I guess Spellbound wasn't concerned with background checks on chaperones.

"Daniel, you can't be serious."

He looked at me with an earnest expression. "Why not? It's a good deed. The more good deeds, the better."

"It won't be seen as a good deed by the boys at the dance," I argued. "Their dates will spend the whole night ogling you instead of getting felt up by them."

"I hadn't really thought about that angle." He scratched his head, thinking. "I've already volunteered. I can't back out now."

"Why don't you find someone to fill in for you?" Someone unattractive and unavailable.

His turquoise eyes brightened. "I have an idea. Why don't you come as my date? Then the girls will leave me alone."

I stifled a laugh. If he thought having me on his arm would keep girls from lusting after him, he knew far less about women than I realized.

"I don't think that's a good idea," I said. Hormonal girls aside, the thought of attending a dance with Daniel struck me as a very bad idea. For me. Although I'd attended my senior prom with a friend, it wasn't the memorable evening that film and television had led me to believe it would be. I had no reason to think the Spellbound dance would be any different.

"Come on," Daniel said, warming to the idea. "It'll give you a chance to wear a gown. I'll even pay for it." He looked at me, his expression softening. "I'd love to see you dressed up."

My heart fluttered. My head screamed at me to say no, but I heard my mouth say, "Okay. I'll do it." Stupid, disloyal mouth.

Daniel slapped a hand on the table. "Great. I'll pick you up at six. Drop by Ready-to-Were and tell Ricardo to show you the gown section."

"Do you need to come with me?"

He shook his head. "I'm pretty sure I still have an account there from when I used to…" His mouth set in a straight line. "Just tell him to bill me."

I had a feeling I knew what Daniel was going to say. He used to lavish attention on women, buying them gowns and flowers from Petals. Now he was buying me a gown, not to mention he'd done several generous things for me already. Wildflowers, fixing up Sigmund, the pot on my mantel. Friendly gestures or old habits? I didn't know. Part of me didn't want to know.

"Mr. Starr," a little boy said. I hadn't even heard him approach. He stepped up to the table with a handful of coins. "How many cups can I get for this?"

Daniel beamed. He was so pleased to help someone. He counted out the coins in the boy's hand. "Five cups. Would you like me to help you carry them?"

"Yes, please," the little boy said. "My mom said not to come back unless I brought the angel with me."

Daniel and I exchanged looks.

"I guess it's a good idea that you're coming with me tomorrow night," he said finally.

I was glad he thought so, because I wasn't so sure.

CHAPTER 12

Lucy met me outside Ready-to-Were. She looked as excited as I felt.

"Gowns," she exclaimed. "Usually the only time I get to shop for gowns is when Mayor Knightsbridge has a fundraiser. I'd much rather choose a gown for you."

"You were the first person I thought of," I said. Lucy had impeccable taste. Between the fairy and Ricardo, the stylish wereferret, I was sure to find the best dress in Spellbound.

We entered the shop and Ricardo caught wind of us immediately. The wereferret rushed over and engulfed us in a group hug.

"My lovelies," he said. "I am ever so happy to see you. What brings you in?"

"I'm a bystander," Lucy practically shouted. "She has a date with Daniel."

I quickly shushed her. "It is not a date. Don't start spreading rumors."

Lucy rolled her eyes. "Fine. It's a pretend date, but still. And it has to look good. Remind Daniel what he's missing."

Ricardo rubbed his hands together. "You have come to the right place. Ricardo is very good at sending the signals."

"Daniel said to put it on his tab," I said. "Does he have a tab?"

Ricardo's brow lifted. "I see. Yes, he does. He hasn't used it on anyone else in quite some time, though."

Lucy disappeared between the racks of gowns. She emerged with a pile of dresses about a foot deep. When I said she had the strength of a dozen men, I wasn't kidding.

"I'll put these in the dressing room," she said. "I've chosen all of your best colors and several different necklines."

It felt odd to be trying on gowns. I couldn't remember the last time I'd even worn a dress in the human world. I tended to wear sweatpants and T-shirts in my apartment and trousers and a dress shirt to work. Dresses rarely enter the equation.

I avoided looking at myself in the magic mirror. For some reason, I didn't want to face what I knew Daniel would see tonight. It wasn't that I was ashamed of my body or anything, but he was an angel. A perfectly formed angel. He never had a hair out of place or a muscle that didn't flex. He was physical perfection, pure and simple. How could I possibly measure up to that?

Lucy pulled the curtain aside and poked her head in. "What's taking so long? Ricardo and I have tried on ten things already."

I laughed. "Why are you trying on clothes?"

"Ricardo wanted to show off his new animal print line." She fluttered into the dressing area and I noticed her outfit. Her mini dress was covered in paw prints. "Are those bear claws?"

"No, silly," she said. "They're ferret feet."

"Okay," I said slowly. Somehow, that was one fashion trend I did not see taking off. I changed into the first gown.

As usual, I marveled as the magical clothing molded to my body. It never ceased to amaze me.

"It's pretty," Lucy said, tilting her head. "But I think you can do better. Try the purple one."

"Really?"

"Purple is one of your best colors," she said. "With your dark hair and light eyes, purple accentuates all of your positives."

I wasn't convinced, but I did as I was told. I trusted Lucy's judgment in all things sartorial.

I studied myself in the magic mirror. I couldn't find fault with a single stitch. Once again, Ricardo's clothing made my body unrecognizable.

"It's amazing," I breathed.

Lucy folded her arms and gave me a smug smile. "Told you so. This is perfect for you."

I craned my neck, trying to locate the price tag. If Daniel was paying, I didn't want to spend too much.

"What are you doing?" Lucy asked.

When I told her, she threw her head back and laughed. "Daniel has more money than half of Spellbound put together. Don't you dare look at that price tag."

"He doesn't even work," I said. "How does he have so much money?"

"When you've lived here as long as he has, you have plenty of time to amass your fortune. He wasn't always this Daniel, remember?"

That was true. He was a fallen angel for a reason. It was just still unclear to me what exactly those reasons were. Other than being a well-known womanizer, I didn't know what his alleged crimes were.

I turned so that I could examine myself from the back in the mirror. The view was just as alluring from that perspective. "I never knew my butt was so round."

Lucy shrugged. "It's probably not. That's just the magic of Ricardo's fabrics."

A magical butt. Who didn't want that?

"Are you sure I should try on the rest of these?" I asked. "I have about twenty here."

Lucy shook her head adamantly. "When you find the one you want, you know it. No need to mess around with the rest."

I couldn't agree more. Unfortunately, the dress wasn't like Daniel. It didn't have a say in the matter.

Ricardo beamed when he saw me emerge from the dressing room in the purple gown. "I knew you would choose that one. I should have just had it ready for you at the outset."

Lucy placed an arm around me. "That's why she brings me. Now if only I had a reason to wear a gown."

"Thank you so much, both of you," I said. "I'm nervous about tonight, but having a beautiful dress means I've already won half the battle."

"Watch out for those high school girls," Ricardo said. "A few of them have come in here for dresses and they are meaning business."

"What you mean?"

Ricardo gave me a knowing look. "You'll see."

My high school prom in the human world was held in the ballroom of a major hotel chain. At the time, we thought it was the height of sophistication. No school cafeteria dance for us! No siree. We were too fancy for linoleum floors. Now, stepping inside the Spellbound High School dance, I felt like a fool. There was no comparison. The decor was tasteful yet still managed to feel special. The ceiling and walls twinkled like we were in the stars' embrace.

Every head seemed to swivel in our direction when we entered the room. Granted, Daniel was hard to ignore with his impressive height and broad shoulders, not to mention those eye-catching wings. Beside him, I looked like a strange growth on his arm that required immediate medical attention.

Darcy Minor came hustling over the moment she spotted us. "Thank you so much for doing this. You have no idea how difficult it is to find good help. You say the words 'school event' and everyone suddenly has unbreakable plans."

"Happy to be here," Daniel said. "Happy to be anywhere as long as I have this one by my side." He gave my waist a tight squeeze.

What was he doing?

Darcy shot us a quizzical look before something drew her attention across the room.

"I see you, Caleb Humphrey," Darcy yelled, and moved swiftly toward the punch bowl to interrupt a spiking attempt.

"You don't have to pretend for Darcy's sake," I said, once she was out of earshot. "It's for the benefit of the young girls, remember?" And probably a few young guys as well.

He pulled me closer and pressed his lips to my ear. "May as well make it believable. I haven't had a date in ages. Let's have fun with it."

My heart hammered in my chest. This evening was going to be torture for me. For Daniel, having me as his date was self-preservation. For me, putting as much distance between us was self-preservation. Why did I say yes?

A young woman approached us, holding two cups of punch. Her dress was more revealing than I would've dared to wear at her age, with a thigh-high split and an off-the-shoulder bodice. Her curls were piled on top of her head in the style of a Grecian goddess. Her makeup was so thick, it was like a second layer of skin. Why were these girls in such a rush to grow up? They lived in Spellbound, where they had umpteen decades to act like adults. I wanted to do a spell that slowed the teens down.

She offered a cup to Daniel. "Mr. Starr, I thought you might be thirsty. I saw you flying overhead earlier today. It's a nice view, from beneath you." She lowered her gaze, her dark lashes fluttering.

I threw up a little in my mouth. Before I could stop myself, I wrapped my arm around Daniel's waist.

"Thank you so much, honey," I said, adopting my most condescending tone. "Which grade are you in? We'll be sure to tell your teacher what a polite girl you are." I looked up at Daniel and smiled. "Such excellent manners."

The young woman scowled at me. "Why are you here? Didn't you get the memo that we don't have witches in this school?"

She was right. Witches attended the academy. It reminded me of the different schools in Lemon Grove. Your options were public school, private school, and Catholic school.

"Miss Hart is my date this evening," Daniel said pointedly. "She's not here as a student. She's a grown woman." He flashed me an endearing smile. "Very grown-up. One of the qualities I love about her."

The young woman scrunched her nose. "That's one of the things you like most about her? How lame." She snatched the cup out of his hand and stomped off.

He winked at me. "That went well, don't you think?"

"We should probably circulate," I said. "Don't we need to make sure the students are on their best behavior?"

"As long as we do it together." His hand slid into mine and squeezed. "I need you by my side tonight. Don't go wandering off with a sexy satyr. Chances are he's too young for you."

My insides tingled. There was no chance of disappearing with anyone in the world. Not while Daniel was touching me. I tried in vain to clear my head. Our pretend relationship was blurring the carefully drawn lines of our friendship.

We stalked the perimeter, investigating dark corners and sniffing drinks for contraband. We managed to remove a bottle of Scorpion's Tail from a group of werewolves in the corridor before returning to the dance floor.

The band was decent for a school event. They played the right variation of fast and slow songs.

The room suddenly darkened as the music slowed and the starlight increased in intensity. The effect was stunning and, although I hated to admit it, very romantic. Beneath our feet, white clouds swelled. Some kind of spell to make it seem as though we floated on a cloud. It was a far cry from the fog machine back at Lemon Grove High School. I noticed a couple of teachers on the dance floor and realized I was looking at Lara and her new boyfriend, the gym teacher. The pixie was engulfed in his arms, swaying in time to the music, and it would've been a sweet scene had I not known how much Thom was hurting.

Daniel extended his hand. "I think it's time for a dance, don't you?"

My knees nearly buckled. Daniel wanted to dance with me. It was difficult enough to fly with him, but this would be worse. Dancing felt more intimate—it was such a sensual movement. When he flew with me in his arms, I was usually hanging on for dear life. Dancing within kissing distance of him would jumpstart a different fear. One I didn't want to address. Nonetheless, I felt myself gliding into his arms and moving to the music. His one hand rested on the small of my back while his other hand gripped mine. When he smiled down at me, I felt like the only person in the world. His gaze was like the sun shining down on me, warming me. Heat coursed through my veins.

It's just pretend, I told myself. But the truth was that it was only pretend for him, not for me.

Daniel's hand moved from my back to caress my hair. I shivered slightly. Now what was he doing?

He lowered his mouth to my ear. "Just play along. We're surrounded by cheerleaders. The blonde propositioned me outside the restroom."

The restroom? I'd only gone in for two minutes. He managed to have a girl proposition him that quickly? No wonder he felt entitled to run through women like my fork through cake. There seemed to be no shortage of females willing to take their chances with him. I guess I was no different. Maybe when Daniel looked at them, it was like the sun shining on their faces too. Who was I to say their feelings were less worthy than mine?

Before I could respond, his fingers gently tipped up my chin. When his lips met mine, every nerve in my body reacted. I melted against him. Resistance was futile. The kiss went longer and deeper than I expected. My fingers drifted to the nape of his neck. When we broke apart, I thought I saw a hint of surprise in his eyes. I didn't know how to interpret it.

"Ew, save it for the privacy of your own home," the blond cheerleader sneered. "No one wants to be subjected to your PDA."

My cheeks flamed.

"I think we need to separate you two," a male voice joked. Lara's boyfriend, the gym teacher.

"I thought we were here to keep tabs on the kids," Lara joined in. "Too much pregaming, maybe?"

"I'm Petros," he said, shaking Daniel's hand and then

mine. "I'm the gym teacher here." His arm was around Lara's tiny waist. They radiated happiness.

"Daniel Starr and this is my date, Emma Hart."

Lara's expression darkened. "Hart? You're the one defending Thom."

"I am," I said. "That's the job of a public defender."

"He needs to stay out of her house," Petros said. "It's not cool. She's been afraid to walk in the house after work in case he's there."

I didn't want to get into an argument. Thom insisted that Lara had planted those 'stolen' items in his house and I was willing to give him the benefit of the doubt. I hadn't been able to drum up a motive for Lara, but now I wondered whether she was trying to get a reaction from Petros. Maybe she wanted to play the role of damsel in distress so that he could play the role of knight in shining armor.

"Emma's not here to talk about the case," Daniel said. "I volunteered to be here and she was kind enough to accompany me."

Lara took Petros by the hand and guided him toward the dance floor where a couple of centaurs were getting carried away with body slams. Petros blew his whistle and my hands flew instinctively to cover my ears. I waited for the shrill sound, but it never came. I glanced over to see the two centaurs sitting calmly on their haunches. A magic whistle? Why was I not surprised?

"I'm sorry about that," I said to Daniel. "Thom seems like a nice guy, but Lara says he stole from her house and he insists she's framing him because of a bad breakup." As always, the truth probably lay somewhere in between.

He entwined his fingers with mine. "Welcome to the Bad Reputation Club. Meetings are every day and always."

I instinctively pulled away my hand. The intimate gesture overwhelmed me.

132

"Hey," he said and I heard the concern in his voice. "We're friends, right?"

I faltered. "We are…whatever you want us to be."

He grinned. "That's a funny way of saying yes. Must be a human thing."

"Must be," I said, and quickly glanced away so that he couldn't see my tears. Movement across the room distracted me. "I think that succubus is about to inhale her date," I said, pointing to a dark corner of the room, where the students' hormones were clearly getting the better of them.

Daniel puffed out his chest, Superman-style. "Time to blow the holy trumpet. That'll get their attention."

"If you don't move quickly," I warned, "I think she's about to blow *his* trumpet."

CHAPTER 13

"Good, you're back," Gareth said, gliding toward me. "Your friends have been camped out here for an hour. If I hear the word 'awesome' one more time, I'm going to find a way to produce vomit."

On cue, three heads poked out of the living room.

"You're home! How was the dance?" Begonia asked. She gasped at the sight of my gown. "Your dress is so pretty."

I stroked the deep, purple material. "It is, isn't it?" I held up the bottle of Scorpion's Tail. "And I managed to bring home a trophy. We confiscated this from a couple of werewolves."

Begonia plucked the bottle from my hand and popped off the lid.

"Should I get glasses or can we just drink from the bottle?" I asked.

"Millie needs a glass," Sophie said. "She doesn't share drinks. We even bought her a mug that says 'no, you can't have a sip' for her birthday last year."

Millie groaned. "You always make such a big deal about it."

"I'm not a fan of germs either," I said. "I'll get the glasses."

"You'd share a bottle with Daniel," Begonia said, following me into the kitchen. "I bet angel germs are acceptable." She smiled coyly. "Maybe even encouraged."

I took four glasses from the cabinet and set them on the counter while Begonia poured the drinks. Sophie and Millie joined us in the kitchen.

"Did you get to dance with Daniel?" Sophie asked. "You did, didn't you?"

I nodded and took a swig of the cheap alcohol so that I didn't have to elaborate.

"We don't have dances at the academy," Millie complained. "It's not fair."

Sophie studied me. "You don't look too happy, Emma. Is something wrong? Was Daniel on his best behavior?"

I laughed. "With me? Always." No matter how much I wished that he wasn't.

"Then what's the matter?" Millie asked.

I opened my mouth to speak, but the emotional knot in my throat stopped me.

Begonia spoke for me. "He's her spirit animal."

I wasn't sure that an angel qualified as a spirit animal, but I agreed with the sentiment.

Millie's brow furrowed. "And? What's wrong with that? Having a spiritual guide in your life sounds like a good thing."

Begonia came over and hugged me. Of all the remedial witches, she seemed the most in tune to my emotions.

"The problem isn't that Daniel's her spirit animal," Begonia said, emitting a soft sigh. "The problem is you're not supposed to want to ride your spirit animal."

"Oh," Millie said. "Right."

I cast my gaze to the floor. As much as I wanted to deny it, I knew it was true. I had the hots for my spirit animal.

"What are you going to do about it?" Sophie asked.

"Nothing," I replied. "Fallen angel, remember? Determined to restore his shiny halo. How can I interfere with such lofty goals? It's selfish." I gulped down more Scorpion's Tail to numb the pain. "Besides, just because I might have feelings for him doesn't mean he feels the same."

"You wouldn't be the first witch to fall for him," Millie said.

"No, but she'd be the first one to develop a genuine friendship with him first," Begonia said. "He seems to dote on her." She looked at me. "He does, you know. You might not see it, but we've all known him longer."

"It's only because he feels guilty," I insisted. "If it weren't for him, I wouldn't be trapped in Spellbound."

"I don't think it's guilt," Begonia said. "He goes out of his way for you. That's not the Daniel Starr we know."

"He bought me this dress," I said, spreading the fabric of the skirt. "He has an account at Ready-to-Were from when he used to *dote* on his other female companions. On the contrary, I think he very much *is* the Daniel Starr you know."

"I'm sorry, Emma," Sophie said. "It seems like we all suffer from romantic rejection in our group."

"Not me," Begonia said. "Claude is wonderful."

"Not me either," Millie said. "I'm not putting myself out there for anyone. Then I can't be rejected."

"No risk, no reward," I murmured. A phrase my grandfather was fond of saying, along with 'youth is wasted on the young.'

"So where's your reward then?" Millie demanded.

I met her accusatory gaze. "I didn't say I've taken the necessary risk." I inhaled sharply. "And I don't plan to anytime soon."

I didn't want to talk about Daniel anymore. I felt a small pang in my heart every time his name was mentioned.

"You must be tired," Sophie said. "We'll go. We just wanted to ask about the dance."

"Thanks," I said. "It was sweet of you to wait for me. I really do appreciate it." I didn't have friends like these in the human world. I was more grateful for them than they realized.

"Ask them to stay for a sleepover," Gareth urged, materializing behind me. "Girls love that stuff."

I gave him a quizzical look. Gareth was encouraging me to invite three witches to spend the night? He must've truly felt sorry for me.

"Would you like to sleep over tonight?" I asked. "I have plenty of space."

"Tell them you'll make oatcakes for breakfast," Gareth said, and then quickly thought better of it. "No, forget it. Cooking isn't your strong suit."

Begonia performed a little happy dance, spilling half of her drink on the floor. Magpie rushed over to lap it up.

"We'd love to," she said. "Wouldn't we, girls?"

In truth, I thought the sleepover was a good idea. I desperately needed to take my mind off the dance—off Daniel, specifically—and there was no better cure for a rejection hangover than the company of true friends.

"I call the chintz bedroom," Millie said.

"And I call the rest of this bottle," Begonia said with a laugh.

I fell asleep to the sound of their laughter about an hour later. It was music to my ears.

The dwarf was gazing at the coffin when I arrived. Even from the back, she looked like her mother. Wide body and stout legs. The crunch of leaves beneath my feet gave me away. Trixie turned her head toward the sound.

"How often do you come here?" I asked, joining her beside the casket. Freddie looked exactly the same as the last time I'd been here. Not that I expected anything different.

"This is only the second time," she said. "I came to the vigil because I didn't believe it until I saw it with my own two eyes."

"I suppose you've spoken to the sheriff about Freddie's case."

"We've had a few conversations," she said cryptically. "He's not the smartest man in any room."

I was inclined to agree, but, at this point, I wasn't sure whether Trixie was friend or foe.

"I heard you met my mother recently," Trixie said. "Caused quite the scene."

"I think you'll find that Lady Sparkles caused the scene, not me." Technically.

"Lady Sparkles." Trixie giggled. "Mother talks about her often. I think it's an alternate persona."

I pictured the elderly witch clinging to the ceiling. "My alternate persona is far less demonic."

"I've been debating whether to bring the kids to see Uncle Freddie. I think he might upset them. They're used to him jolly and laughing."

"How old are your kids?" I asked.

"Mary is seven and Dell is nine," she replied. "My husband says not to bring them, that this could be their last image of him." She pressed her forehead against the glass.

"It's a beautiful casket," I said. "It stands to reason that whomever cursed him cared about him."

Trixie ran a hand along the side of the glass. "It is rather nice, isn't it? And he's holding flowers. I thought that was a nice touch."

"What's your relationship like with Freddie?"

Trixie shrugged. "He's my little brother. I'd say our rela-

tionship is fairly typical. I boss him around and he listens."
She chuckled softly. "Not much different from my relationship with my husband."

"Your mother said Freddie came twice a week to visit her.
How about you?"

Trixie gave me a serious case of side eye. "I'm a mother
and a wife," she said. "I also work a full-time job. Freddie has
plenty of time to visit."

The tension was palpable. This was clearly a sore spot
between siblings.

"So I take it you don't have a set visiting schedule."

Trixie shook her head. "There are days when I'm lucky I
take a shower. My husband is all for equal rights between all
genders and all supernaturals, but he still seems to prefer
that I do the dragon's share of the cooking and cleaning." She
paused. "And child-rearing and the finances. It doesn't leave a
lot of time for visits to mother."

"I suppose the care home was the only option," I said.

Trixie laughed bitterly. "Not according to Freddie. He
begged me not to put her in the home. He said it would
hasten her demise."

"If it's any consolation," I said, "your mother seems in fine
spirits there."

"I do think she's happy there, but I still feel guilty about it.
There was just no way I could take her in, not with two
young kids, a husband, and a busy schedule. Mother has a
heart condition. What if something happened and no one
was home to help her?"

"I understand," I said.

"Freddie wanted me to take her," she said hotly. "He didn't
seem to get the fact that it made more sense for him to do it.
He lives alone." She hesitated. "We fought about this, as you
probably guessed."

"You and millions of other human families," I said. "Not to diminish your experience, but you're hardly alone in this."

"Freddie said his place was too small and he couldn't afford somewhere bigger. He also wanted to be able to move forward in a relationship. He didn't feel able to do that with mother as his roommate."

"And that's totally understandable, too. I think you did what was best for everyone."

A tear slid down the dwarf's cheek. "Freddie and I had just had another argument about it the week before this happened. He'd gone to see our mother and he wasn't happy when he came home. He ran straight over to me, insisting that we take her out of the home, but I refused."

"Do you know if something happened?"

Trixie stifled a giggle. "I think he caught an elderly gentleman leaving our mother's room and he wasn't thrilled about it. To be honest, I think he was jealous that our ancient mother was getting more action than he was."

"It wasn't a genie by any chance, was it?" I cringed at the thought of Agnes and Estella sharing the sex-crazed genie.

"He started raving about mother's heart condition and how this can't be good for her. I told him that I thought it was great for her and that just made him angry." Her expression softened. "That was our last conversation. Can you believe it? Now I have to talk to him through a glass wall and I don't even know if he can hear me."

"How did you end the conversation? Did you agree to remove her from the home?"

Trixie shook her head vigorously. "Absolutely not. Nothing had changed. Freddie was still a bachelor and I'm still a harassed wife and mother. He threatened to drive over there and remove her himself."

"But he didn't do that," I said.

"Of course he didn't. That would mean mother moving in

with him and he wasn't prepared to give up his bachelor lifestyle."

"From what I've heard, Freddie wasn't really comfortable with the bachelor lifestyle." In fact, his story reminded me of Killian's, the vampire I met in Pandora's office. "It sounded to me like Freddie really wanted to settle down and get married."

"Well, I don't think that's likely to happen."

"Obviously not while he's under the curse."

She looked at me askance. "Not just that. I'm talking about Heidi."

I squinted. "What does Heidi have to do with it?"

Trixie caressed the glass. "I'm sorry to do this to you, brother," she said softly, before turning to me. "Freddie is madly in love with Heidi."

The news floored me. "Heidi has a boyfriend. She's been dating Paul for a year."

Trixie's eyes closed. "Freddie didn't discuss it often. Just an offhand comment now and again. But I know my brother and I know what's in his heart. It gutted him to see Heidi with Paul."

My mind was spinning. "But Freddie was a regular on the dating scene. He was looking for a girlfriend."

Trixie focused on me. "It was only a distraction from the pain, I think. Make no mistake, he loves Heidi more than anything. He was devastated when she agreed to go out with Paul."

"Why did he never say anything? They're such good friends."

"Exactly," Trixie said. "He didn't want to risk losing the friendship. It's the most meaningful relationship he's ever had." The tears began to flow freely as Trixie unburdened herself. "I think he kept waiting for Paul to mess up. Then he expected Heidi to seek solace with him, but it just hasn't happened."

My heart ached for Freddie. How must it have felt for him to see the woman he loved day in and day out, knowing she was with someone else? No wonder he had no luck in the dating department. He didn't really want to meet anyone— because he already had.

CHAPTER 14

ON THE DAY OF TRIAL, Thom met me at my office and we walked over to the Great Hall. He continually fussed with his tie to the point where I ordered him to take it off.

"But you said I needed a tie," he objected, clutching the sliver of blue fabric.

"Not the way you're wearing it." I undid the knot and removed the offending item from his collar. "It's too distracting."

"Sorry," he mumbled. "Just nervous is all."

"You're not the only one."

The doors to the Great Hall opened and we walked down the aisle to our assigned table. Across from us was the prosecutor, a wizard called Rochester.

"We meet again, Miss Hart," he said.

"The odds were pretty good, considering I'm the public defender."

His smile faded and he returned to his seat.

"All rise for Judge Lee Millville," the bailiff said.

We continued to stand as the judge strode into the room. He was on the taller side for a dwarf, which wasn't saying much. His hair was a thick, silver helmet and his nose reminded me of a triangle with rounded edges.

The doors opened and Lara fluttered into the room. Thankfully, her boyfriend didn't join her. Thom would have been devastated to see Petros at his trial.

Lara took a seat at the back of the room, out of Thom's view.

The judge opened the proceedings and Rochester and I gave our opening statements. Lara was the first witness called to the stand. She barely glanced at Thom as she answered the prosecutor's questions.

"And what is your relationship with the defendant?" Rochester asked.

Lara straightened. "We were previously in a romantic relationship." She offered a few more details about their time together and the fact that she was now in a new relationship with her co-worker.

During her entire testimony, Thom never once took his eyes off of her. When she finished, she returned to the back of the room, refusing to meet his gaze as she passed him.

Next Sheriff Hugo entered the room to offer his testimony.

"We found the five stolen items together in a trunk at the base of the defendant's bed," he said.

"What made you look there?" the judge asked.

"It was partially open, as though the defendant knew we were coming and had attempted to remove the contraband before we arrived."

Despite my best efforts, it wasn't looking good for my client. Finally, it was Thom's turn to testify. I gave his hand a quick squeeze as he stood to take his seat beside the judge.

"Mr. Farley," Rochester began. "You've heard the testimony here today. Given the facts in evidence, do you still purport that you were framed by Miss Honeycutt?"

Thom's gaze drifted to Lara and I could tell from his pained expression that he was about to lose it. He covered his face with his hands.

"I did it, okay?" he blurted. "I committed burglary. I stole those five things."

I heard a gasp and quickly realized that it came from me. My hand whipped across my mouth.

The judge tilted his head, examining Thom. "Why those five things, Mr. Farley? There was nothing of value there."

Thom heaved a sigh. "The vase was the first thing we ever bought together. To me, it represented our future. She broke up with me. Why would she want that vase displayed on her mantel? How could it not remind her of me every time she looked at it?"

A blanket of silence covered the Great Hall. As his lawyer, I knew I had to stop him from incriminating himself, even though the human part of me recognized his need to unburden himself.

"Your Honor, my client has misspoken," I said.

The judge fixed me with his hard stare. "He seems to be speaking just fine to me." He looked at Thom. "Continue."

"The knitted hat was made by my grandmother for Lara. My grandmother died last year, before we broke up. It made me upset to think about something so meaningful still in her possession." He turned his focus to Lara. "You said you didn't love me anymore. Why would you want these things? Why would you want something that just serves to remind you of me?"

From her place in the back of the Great Hall, Lara piped up. "That's precisely the reason I kept them. Because they reminded me of you. Of our time together, when we still loved each other." She fluttered to the front of the room, tears brimming in her eyes. "When I look at those things, they make me happy because they remind me of happier times. I know you think they should make me sad, but they don't. And when they were gone, I noticed. I missed them." Her voice shook with emotion and I felt my own throat tightening in response.

The judge banged his gavel, ordering silence.

"We've already heard from you, Miss Honeycutt," the judge said. "Let us hear from the defendant now. Carry on, Mr. Farley."

"The book of poems I took because they were sitting on the table in front of you the first time you ever told me you loved me. I thought maybe reading the poems had made you emotional enough to say that. You'd always seemed so guarded before then. And the horse…" He trailed off.

"I understand," Lara said. "You carved it for me." She glanced at the judge. "Horses are my favorite animal."

"I only took one thing at a time," he admitted. "Each time I thought of something, I went over to your house and took it. It made me angry to think that you got to enjoy those memories. I wanted to strip them all bare, leave you with nothing to remember me by."

"Thom," she said. "I would never want to erase you from my life. You've been so important to me. I'd never been in love before I met you. You showed me that it was okay to be vulnerable with someone. I never, ever want to forget that."

Thom hung his head in shame.

"That's quite enough, Miss Honeycutt," the judge said. "You may step down, Mr. Farley."

Thom slumped in the seat next to me. "I'm sorry," he whispered.

I placed my hand over his. "It's okay."

"We have a confession and the evidence to support it," the judge said. "Therefore, I sentence you, Thom Farley, to ten years in Spellbound prison."

I jumped to my feet. "Your Honor, ten years seems

extreme for five items of sentimental value. My client is clearly not a threat to society."

"It doesn't matter that he's not a threat to society," the judge replied. "What matters is that he committed the crime and the law clearly states what the penalty is."

"But you have discretion when it comes to sentencing," I insisted. "Thom is not at risk to be a repeat offender. Even the victim doesn't want him to serve time for what he did." I craned my neck to see the pixie. "Isn't that right, Lara?"

The judge peered down at me. "You are a lawyer, Miss Hart, are you not? You of all people should understand that the law is the law. They are in place for a reason and they cannot be disregarded simply because you find the defendant to be a nice guy."

"But what about the spirit of the law?" I asked. "The law is judging my client too harshly for his actions. It's quite clear from the circumstances that my client is not going to be burglarizing the homes of other Spellbound residents." I knew I was overstepping, but I was on a roll. "Everyone in this room is aware of the curse. Why was an entire town cursed for the actions of one or maybe a few other people? No one knows, but I assure you that no one here thinks the punishment fits the crime. It's too extreme. If the enchantress knocked on the doors of two residents and they both rejected her, why is it fair that the entire population of what was then known as Ridge Valley should suffer the consequences for generations to come? You're asking my client to suffer disproportionately, the way everyone in this town has suffered as a result of the curse."

My impassioned speech seemed to have no effect on the judge.

"Your Honor," Rochester said, and I braced myself for his objection. "I know this is unorthodox, but I would like to throw my weight behind Miss Hart's request."

I nearly keeled over from shock.

The judge stared at Rochester, baffled by his statement. "You represent the people, Rochester. Have you taken leave of your senses?"

"With all due respect, sir, I think the people would agree that we need to take a closer look at our laws and the harsh sentences that often accompany them. Perhaps Miss Hart is correct and it is, indeed, time for a change. Why are we punishing residents so harshly? She's right. We all believe the curse was an extreme and unfair response."

"The curse is precisely why we have these harsh penalties in place," the judge said. "The residents here live far beyond the typical human life. Some are immortal. What good is a two-year sentence for a vampire? That's no retribution or deterrent."

He made a fair point. Still, I felt strongly that it was time to re-examine the sentencing guidelines of Spellbound.

"I suggest you take your concerns to the town council," the judge said. "Perhaps they will consider creating a commission to study the current guidelines and see where improvements might be made." The judge eyed me carefully. "Perhaps they might even ask you to serve on this commission."

Beside me, Thom's hand shook with fear. A commission could take years to make its findings. Even a positive outcome would do Thom no good today.

"Your Honor," Lara said, rising to her feet. "I'd like to revise my testimony."

Thom and I exchanged confused glances.

"The time for testimony has passed," the judge said. "The verdict has been rendered."

"Then unrender it." Lara rushed to the bench. "Please, I lied. I need to tell the truth."

"You do realize there is a penalty for lying to a judge," the judge said archly.

Rochester held up his finger. "True, Your Honor, but remember that the sentencing guidelines are much more flexible in that situation." He gave her a knowing look. "I do believe there is an option for no time served."

The judge sighed. "Go on then. Give us your new version of events." The judge seemed resigned to our obvious conspiracy.

"I hid the items in Thom's house," she said. "He didn't steal anything. I knew what they meant to him. That's why I chose those five things. I framed him."

Thom closed his eyes, absorbing her statement. We all knew it was a lie, but no one cared. Tears pricked my eyes.

"And I lied to protect Lara," Thom added.

The judge groaned. "Based on the new evidence, I hereby declare Thom Farley a free brownie. The charges are dropped and the case is dismissed."

Beside me, Thom burst into tears. I put a comforting arm around his shoulders.

"As for you," the judge said to Lara. "I sentence you to six months of community service."

"Any specific type?" Rochester asked.

The judge smiled faintly. "Six months in the presence of teenagers. It seems to me that's quite enough punishment for anyone."

I understood then what the judge was doing. As a teacher, Lara already spent six months a year with teenagers. She was essentially serving no sentence at all. My heart swelled.

The judge slammed down his gavel. Thom reached over and hugged me. Lara turned from the bench and approached our table.

"I forgive you, Thom. I'm sorry for all the trouble I caused."

Thom wiped away a stray tear. "I forgive you, too. And I'm sorry I didn't spend enough time with you. You deserve someone who dotes on you."

Lara gave him an affectionate squeeze on the arm as she fluttered from the room.

Rochester closed the gap between us. "I'd like to be involved in the request for a commission," he said. "I have a lot of experience with the town council. I do hope you'll consider me an asset."

"Absolutely," I said. "I couldn't do it alone." Nor did I want to. It seemed to me when there were so many good people around you, why would you want to do anything alone?

"Thank you," Thom said. The relief was evident in his eyes. "Never in a million years did I think I was walking out of here a free brownie."

"Not entirely free," I said. "There is the little matter of our deal."

He tapped his fingers on the table. "Thursday night. Speed dating. It's already on my calendar."

I wasn't sure if he'd successfully meet someone, but a fresh start was all any of us could hope for.

CHAPTER 15

I SAT ON THE BED, leaning against the pillow and flipping through one of the books on the town's history that I'd received from Juliet, the Amazon who owned the bookstore.

"What are you reading?" Gareth floated into the room and peered over my shoulder.

"You really need to learn how to knock," I said.

"I'd love to learn how to knock," he said. "Is there a section in that book called Poltergeisting for Dummies?"

"Anything to avoid a Grey sister, huh?" I asked. "It's not that kind of book. I'm just brushing up on Spellbound. I think it would be helpful to know more about the different paranormal residents and their individual cultures."

"The best way to learn about a culture is to experience it firsthand," Gareth said. "If you want to know more about vampires, then you need to hang out with more vampires. It's as simple as that."

"For someone with stacks of books in his home and office, you're fairly dismissive of reading."

"It depends on *why* you're reading," he said. "If you're reading to learn more about the culture, then I think your time would be better spent among them. If you're reading to learn more about our history to be sure we're not doomed to repeat it, then, by all means, carry on."

"I had no idea you had such strong opinions on the matter." I snapped the book shut. "Did you know that the werewolves didn't always live in the Pines, the Oaks, and the Birches?"

"Aye, Spellbound has evolved over time, as does any town."

"I'm also looking for information on a deck of cards," I said.

"What kind of cards?" Gareth asked. "Are you thinking about having another type of game night?" I'd recently hosted poker night, which quickly devolved into a hunt for a missing werewolf. Despite the chaos of the evening, everyone seemed eager to give game night another try.

"No, when I went to see Agnes at the Spellbound Care Home, she started to read my cards. We didn't get to finish, though. I was trying to see if I could figure out what the cards meant."

Gareth drifted into a seated position on the bed. "What did they look like?"

"Mine had a witch, a werewolf, a vampire, an owl, an angel, and a sun. Does that sound at all significant to you?"

Gareth shook his head. "Vampires don't tend to dabble in readings. When you're immortal, you're more willing to take each day as it comes."

Somehow, that made sense to me. "I looked in the index and skimmed the pages, but I didn't see anything about cards."

"You should go and talk to Juliet again," he suggested. "She's a gold mine of information, not just about town history."

"Do you think the cards are a witch thing?" I asked. If that was the case, then I could ask Ginger or possibly even Professor Holmes.

"There are several groups that indulge in card reading," he said. "Or you could go back and see Agnes."

I squeezed my eyes closed. "Against my better instincts, I am planning to go again." I covered my face with my hands. "She stole my wand, Gareth. That old crone got me drunk and stole my wand."

Gareth fell backward in a fit of laughter.

"It's not funny," I insisted. "She turned the entire cafeteria into reptiles and amphibians. I was mortified."

"Oh, I do wish I had been there. Did she at least provide you with information about your coven?"

"Unfortunately not. She'd never heard of a coven that could see ghosts, although she'd heard of owl familiars. That was as much information as she offered." I hesitated. "She told me about Raisa, said I might want to pay her a visit."

Gareth shot to his feet. "Raisa? Is she mad?"

Now my curiosity was piqued. "Why? What's wrong with Raisa?"

"If you thought Agnes was scary and conniving, then do yourself a favor and stay far away from Raisa. At least she has the decency to stay far away from us."

Too late.

"Agnes did mention that Raisa wanted to be forgotten. What do you know about her?"

"Nothing, other than the fact that she's a frightening old hag. I don't think there's anything she could tell you about your coven. You're better off with your nose in the books."

He certainly changed his tune quickly. "You'll be relieved to know Raisa is dead."

"Really?" Gareth seemed surprised.

"I already went to see her and met her ghost…or something. She seemed solid and she could touch everything in her cottage. If you really want to learn about being a ghost, she might be a good resource."

"I'd rather stick a needle in my eye."

I folded my arms. "But that wouldn't hurt because it would go right through you."

"Hmm. Fair point. So did you learn anything else interesting in that book so far?" Gareth asked.

"I learned that Lord Gilder must be very old. He's been the head of your vampire coven since the town's inception."

"That he is," Gareth agreed.

"Has there ever been any opposition to his leadership?"

"Vampires aren't as territorial as, say, werewolves," Gareth said. "Unless there's a serious issue, we're happy to carry on as we are. Lord Gilder has been a strong and fair leader."

"Why does it seem like there are so few female vampires compared with males?" I asked.

"I don't know that there are," Gareth said. "I think it's just that you attract the males. Fresh blood, you see."

Ick. I hated to think of myself as a walking blood bag. "Do you really think that's the only reason Demetrius was interested in me? My newness."

"I couldn't say for certain," he said. "But a unicorn doesn't change its horn overnight. Dem has always been a player and I don't see any reason to think he's ready to settle down now." He eyed me carefully. "Why? Are you reconsidering your decision?"

"No," I said reluctantly. "Just curious." I'd decided to break things off with Demetrius before it became a full-blown dating situation. Not because I didn't like him. I did. As the new girl in town, though, my plate was overloaded.

"It seems Daniel is trying very hard to turn over a new leaf," Gareth said, a hint of amusement in his voice. "How's that going for him?"

"At the moment, he's trouncing Darcy as the ultimate

volunteer in Spellbound. He's got a finger in every phil-anthropic pot."

"Good for him," Gareth said. "And high time, too."

"I'd like to stay out of his way as much as possible," I admitted. As much as I longed to spend time with Daniel, I knew some time apart was a necessity. The more I was with him, the more I wanted the relationship to progress. I thought of Freddie and his secret love for Heidi and tears welled in my eyes.

Gareth noticed my tears before I could blink them away. "What's the matter? Did I say something wrong?"

"No, no. I was just thinking about Freddie in his endless sleep." I told Gareth about the dwarf's love for Heidi. It wasn't like Gareth could tell anyone, so I knew Freddie's secret would be safe.

"That's rough," he said, rubbing his chin. "I know first-hand what it's like to carry such a heavy secret. Poor lad. Look on the bright side, maybe Heidi and Paul will break up while Freddie's under the curse. Then when he wakes up, Heidi will be free to date him."

"But do we know what Heidi's feelings are for him? Is there a chance that she could view him as more than a friend?"

"There's always a chance," Gareth said.

The gears began clicking in my mind. What if Paul felt threatened by their friendship? Is it possible that Paul played a role in the curse? Maybe the elaborate coffin and affec-tionate touches were done to throw investigators off the trail.

I placed the book on my bedside table and leaped off the bed.

"Where are you off to in such a hurry?" Gareth asked.

"Spellbound Country Club."

"Aren't you supposed to meet the fabulous Fabio today?" he asked. "That is today, right?"

I rounded on him. "Will you stop eavesdropping on every conversation? Yes, that's today, but I have time to drop by the country club on my way into town."

"Why the country club? Are you finally going to address that extra five pounds…?" He trailed off and began to whistle softly to himself.

I narrowed my eyes. "I need to see a satyr about a dwarf." A sentence I never expected to utter.

"Maybe try out some of the equipment while you're there," Gareth called after me.

Extra five pounds, my ass, I thought.

I don't think he means on your ass, Sedgwick chimed in.

I let out an exasperated yell. "For the record, Sedgwick can see and hear you, Gareth. Have fun together. Bye!"

I slammed the door behind me before my owl could escape. Served them both right.

I didn't have too much time, but I couldn't allow my date with Fabio to trump my investigation. The longer Freddie slept, the more dangerous the situation became. Not to mention there was a malicious spell caster on the loose. Spellbound didn't need any more surprises.

A valet greeted me at the entrance to the club and I recognized him from the first time I was here. I'd come to speak with Gareth's friends about him before I'd met him. In fact, the first time I'd met Demetrius was on this very golf course.

"Miss Hart," the valet said, holding open my car door. "Welcome back. Have you finally decided to join?"

"Not today, thanks," I said. "I'm looking for Paul, the trainer. Do you know him?"

"He's usually in the gym until around six. If you take the first hall on your right, you'll find it."

"Thank you." I hustled inside and hoped I didn't run into Heidi. I didn't want to explain why I was here.

The gym was much larger than I expected. While it had some of the typical equipment like weights and ellipticals, it also had items I didn't recognize. Floating ribbons and a string of colorful hoops near the ceiling.

"Hey, you look familiar," a voice said.

Paul. He was in the process of wiping his bare chest down with a towel and, I had to admit, it was a decent view.

"Emma," I reminded him. "We met at Freddie's vigil."

At the mention of Freddie, his expression clouded over. "Yes, that's right." His friendly tone dissipated. "Are you here for a training session?"

"No, I'd like to have a look at the gym here. I'm thinking about joining." And based on his unhappy reaction to Freddie's name, I wanted to probe a little deeper into his feelings about Heidi and Freddie's relationship.

"Great, I can show you around," he said. His mood seemed to lift. He tossed the towel into a nearby laundry basket and prepared to begin the grand tour. "I don't see many witches in here. Which areas of your body are you planning to focus on?"

"Why don't you get too many witches?"

Paul punched a fist into the palm of his hand. His version of a thoughtful gesture. "I don't know. I assume it's because you have spells and stuff to make yourselves look good."

There had to be another reason. I knew for a fact that Begonia and Sophie worked out regularly and that the coven housed an aerobics room in one of their private buildings. Maybe it was the insular nature of the coven at work again.

"Well, I'm new so I don't know too many spells," I admitted, then gave him my best version of a coy look, which probably landed somewhere between drunk and constipated. "I bet you know more spells than I do."

Paul laughed. "Doubtful. I don't mess around much with magic."

Much or not at all? "Really? I thought everyone in Spellbound used magic."

"Unless you're a natural spell caster like you, it's not easy to perform magic. Heidi can do cool stuff with water, but a satyr's skills are generally limited to stuff like winemaking and flute playing." He flexed his bicep. "And looking awesome."

"Do you make wine?"

"Not personally, but my family owns one of the local vineyards. Lenae Winery."

"That's very cool." I didn't even realize Spellbound had vineyards. I learned something new every day.

He circled around me, examining my body. "My suggestion would be a little tightening in certain areas, but nothing insurmountable."

Gee, thanks. "The tour, Paul."

He snapped to attention. "Oh, right." He pointed out various pieces of equipment and gave me the spiel about the benefits of daily exercise. I started to tune out. Hearing about exercise was even worse than doing it.

"Thanks so much, Paul," I interjected. "I need to get moving. I have to head into town. If I have any questions, I'll let you know."

He seemed surprised by my quick exit. "Sure, no problem."

I waved over my shoulder as I hurried out of the gym. His reaction to Freddie's name was interesting, but his statement about not messing around with magic seemed believable. I wasn't sure what to think.

I was so engrossed in my thoughts that I nearly crashed

into Patrick, another employee of the country club that I'd met before.

"Emma Hart," the centaur said, greeting me with a big smile. "I was hoping you'd change your mind about joining."

"I haven't yet," I said apologetically. "I was checking out the gym. Paul was kind enough to give me the full tour."

"The *full* tour?" He arched a thick eyebrow. "Paul, huh? A little surprising."

"Why is that?"

"No offense, but he generally doesn't go for tall girls. He likes the dainty ones."

"He wasn't…" I stopped. "Isn't he in a serious relationship with Heidi?"

Patrick pretended to zip his lips together. "Oops. You didn't hear it from me."

So Paul was a player. Was there any male in this town not chasing multiple women at once?

"I need to run," I said. "It was good to see you again."

"Let me know next time you come by," he said. "I'll show you around the whole club. The gym is the least interesting part."

I couldn't tell if he was hitting on me or just being friendly. I didn't have time to worry about it right now.

"Thanks, I will." I left the club and was surprised to see Sigmund already waiting for me. "How did you know I was leaving?"

The valet grinned. "It's my job, Miss Hart."

And he was damn good at it.

I slid into the driver's seat and sped off toward the town square. So if, as Patrick hinted, Paul was regularly cheating on Heidi, then I didn't see why he'd need Freddie out of the way. True, Paul could still be jealous of their relationship despite his own indiscretions, but it seemed less likely that he'd perform a complicated curse. And it was even less likely he'd take great pains to make sure Freddie was comfortable in his endless sleep. The glass coffin, the pillow, and the flowers—they all suggested that the responsible party cared about Freddie.

I scratched Paul off my mental list and parked the car near the town square.

Fabio and I agreed to meet at the clock tower. I figured he would be easy to spot based on Pandora's description. I told him I'd wear a red flower on my top so that he'd be able to identify me.

He was waiting for me when I arrived. Pandora wasn't kidding. His hair lived up to its reputation. I found myself wanting to run my fingers through it before we'd even been introduced.

"You must be Emma," he said. "You're every bit as beautiful as Pandora said. I assumed she was exaggerating."

A blush crept into my cheeks. His hair wasn't the only attractive thing about him. I could see evidence of his rippling muscles through the thin fabric of his shirt. It must've been very frustrating for the women of Spellbound to have a specimen like this in their midst with no hope of dating him. Naturally, my thoughts turned to Daniel and my heart squeezed. I pushed aside thoughts of the angel and focused my attention on Fabio.

"I've never met a werelion before," I said. I hoped that wasn't a stupid thing to say. Or racist. Yikes, I'd already insulted him and we hadn't even started the date yet.

Fabio grinned, seemingly unoffended. "A werelion virgin. I'm glad I could be the first then."

"So where are we going?" I asked. I prayed that he did not say the casino. I'd had quite enough of gambling for the time being.

"How do you feel about hiking?"

Phew. "That sounds good," I said. "How far is it? Do we need to take a car?"

"Yes, but I have wheels if you don't mind riding with me."

Why would I mind? He led me to where he'd parked and I quickly realized why. Fabio didn't have a car. He had the magical version of a motorcycle. Why was I not surprised?

He patted the section of the seat behind him. "You'll want to hold onto me. I assume that's okay."

With pecs like his, it was more than okay. I slid the helmet over my head. "What about you? Aren't you going to wear a helmet?"

Fabio flipped his hair over his shoulder. "Not with this mane. That would be a crime against nature."

My stomach sank. My gut told me I was about to see why Fabio was still in the market for a love match. I got on the back of the bike and wrapped my arms around him.

"Feels good, right?" he called over his shoulder. As much as I wanted to assume he meant the bike, I was pretty sure he meant his body.

He revved the magical engine and we took off. We rode the motorcycle as far as the foothills to the north. I'd only been as far as the remedial witch hideout, and I certainly hadn't been hiking. Although I liked the outdoors, I was not particularly athletic. Then again, I'd been walking back and forth to town so often before Sigmund arrived that I was probably in good enough shape to hike one of the mountains. Not that I'd offer.

I left my helmet with the bike and we strode toward the base of the nearest hill.

"Do you have a usual trail that you take?" I asked.

"I like to vary it," he said. "I come here so often that I basically know every trail like the back of my paw."

I wondered if he intended to shift into a lion for the hike.

I wasn't sure how comfortable I was with that. Would he recognize me in his lion form or would I be a slab of walking meat? I had to ask to alleviate my nerves.

"So when you hike these trails, do you do it in human form or lion form?"

Fabio grinned. "Not to worry, Emma. I'm happy to take whatever form interests you."

His statement was either very considerate or he'd dated a few women who were partial to bestiality. Oddly, the latter did not surprise me in Spellbound. The culture here was so recognizable, and yet so completely different from the human world.

"I don't mind," I said. As long as you don't eat me.

"You have nice legs," he said, his gaze traveling up from my feet to my hips.

"Thank you. It's probably from all the walking I've been doing."

"Well, whatever it is, keep doing it. It's working for you." His long hair whipped in the wind and I fought the urge to tie it back for him. He didn't strike me as the type of man who wore a ponytail. He seemed to want his hair free flowing.

I trudged up the hill beside him, making small talk. He occasionally pointed out a species of plant or a speck in the distance and offered details. I didn't feel the same level of companionship that I felt with Daniel, but Fabio was proving himself to be decent company. In some ways, that was better. I did not want the angst that came with Daniel. It was nice to have a friend without the romantic underpinnings. Technically, I had that with Gareth too, but somehow it didn't seem the same, probably because he was—you know—dead.

After about an hour of hiking, Fabio stretched out his arms. "I need to loosen up," he said. "Would you mind if I shifted and went for a quick run?"

"Are there no regulations for werelions?" I asked. I was familiar with the shifting ordinances for werewolves. I had no idea if they extended to other shifters.

Fabio gave me an approving nod. "Already up on the rules and regulations, huh? Good for you. I guess that's important for a public defender. To answer your question, we're far enough outside of town that the rules don't get enforced out here."

"It does seem pretty far away from civilization," I said. In a good way.

"Yes, you won't see too many residents out here. There was an incident, maybe ten or so years ago. Two people died on a camping trip. Things like that tend to keep others away."

"Are you talking about the berserkers?" I knew the story from Linsey, the young berserker I defended in a vandalism case. Her father had killed her mother in a murder suicide and a young Linsey had been with them. It was a sad story, but Linsey was doing well, working with children in an after school art program. I was really proud of her.

"Yes, that's the one."

"At the risk of insulting you," I began, "will you recognize me in your animal form? I mean, it's safe for me, right?"

"One hundred percent," Fabio assured me.

He removed his shirt and his pecs were as glorious as his mane. To be honest, I'm pretty sure I stopped breathing for a moment. When he began to unbutton his trousers, I waved my hands emphatically.

"Whoa, what do you think you're doing?"

"Typical witch," he said with a laugh. "Each one more prudish than the last. I'm only undressing to make it easier to shift."

With that, he dropped his trousers and that was how I learned that Fabio went commando. It wasn't information I needed on a first date, especially when I had no intention of moving on to a second date. My conservative mindset faded, however, when he began to shift. So far, I had only seen a werewolf in a half state and it had looked painful and unpleasant. Fabio's shift was effortless, almost graceful. I blinked and the attractive man was replaced by an enormous lion. He silently acknowledged me before racing further up the hill. What a rush.

I thought I'd be nervous on the hillside by myself, but it was actually quite pleasant. There was a light breeze and a wonderful view of the town in the distance. I wanted to ask Daniel if he ever came up here. It seemed like the kind of place he would enjoy. As soon as the thought entered my mind, I berated myself. I had to stop thinking about Daniel. Everywhere I turned, I saw the angel. I wasn't going to be able to exist in this town if I didn't change my mindset.

The sun was warm on my skin and it felt good to be outdoors. Up on the hillside with no paranormals in sight, I could almost pretend I was back in the human world. Nothing around me suggested a magical town hidden from view. My thoughts drifted to my tiny apartment and I wondered what became of it. Did the landlord move my things into storage, what little possessions I owned? I wasn't sure what the legalities were in connection with a missing person, but, since I hadn't paid rent in months, it seemed only fair that he should evict me. I thought about Huey, my stuffed owl, packed away in the storage container under my bed. Truth be told, I'd forgotten about him until recently. Now I missed him like he was a part of me. I ached to hug his soft material to my chest and rub my cheek against the top of his head the way I did when I was a little girl in need of comfort. It was the one thing my grandparents could use as leverage against me. If they wanted me to do something and I refused, they would simply threaten Huey and I would quickly fall into line. Sharp and ruthless negotiators, those two.

I climbed the hill, hoping to catch a glimpse of the human world in the distance. I knew downtown Spellbound was south of here, so I faced the opposite direction. The only view was Mother Nature herself. Peaks and valleys. Blue sky and puffy clouds above. Still, I saw the value in coming here and getting away from it all. In this seemingly borderless landscape, it was easy to forget that I was trapped in a paranormal town forever.

As I reached the peak of the hill, I passed two stone gargoyles. What an odd place for statues. For a split second I thought maybe they were remnants of a previous homestead, but the idea of a house on the edge of a hill this size seemed unlikely.

From this vantage point, I could see downtown Spell-bound nestled in the valley below. It was just as appealing from this height as it was from the ground. I could make out the church spire and the clock tower, the two highest points in town. The entire place looked peaceful and inviting. No wonder an enchantress wandered into Ridge Valley seeking hospitality. Who could blame her?

"What are you doing?" Fabio's voice startled me. I whipped around to see him back in human form, buck-naked and looking at me like I'd just melted down his precious motorcycle and sold it for scrap.

"What's wrong?" His mane was wild and his hands were balled into fists at his side.

"Come down from there right now," he demanded.

I glanced around me with uncertainty. "It's perfectly safe here. Believe me, I'm the last person who would stand too close to the edge. I'm deathly afraid of heights."

He shook his head and beckoned me forward. "That's not what I mean. Don't you know what this place is?"

"The top of a hill?"

"This is Curse Cliff," he said. "This is the spot where the enchantress cursed the town. It's forbidden to stand there."

So in a town full of red tape, the one place that is strictly forbidden has no sign to alert unsuspecting residents?

"Shouldn't there be a sign here that says 'Danger. Keep out?'" Replace 'enchantress' with 'alien' and you had the Spellbound equivalent of Area 51.

"Didn't you see the gargoyles?" he asked, pointing to the two statues.

Oh. Oops.

Anger flashed in his eyes. "You need to get over here now. Her dark energy will be all over you."

Before he turned into a lion and mauled my ass, I dutifully complied.

"I'm sorry," I said. "I went for a walk and this is where I ended up. It's the perfect view of Spellbound."

"Why do you think she chose that spot to cast her evil spell?"

"How do you know for certain? No one is even sure of the curse's origin," I said. "How can anyone possibly know that the cliff is the precise spot where she carried out her revenge?"

"In the werelion pack, we're told from the time we're cubs that we're not allowed on Curse Cliff," Fabio explained. "I can't speak for the other groups in the town. I know that most shifters believe the land beyond the gargoyles is to be avoided." He gave me a look of disgust and I knew with absolute certainty that there would be no second date. In his mind, I was drenched in malevolent energy. Unclean!

We returned to the spot where he'd left his clothes and he began to dress. "It was a mistake to bring you here. We should've gone to Perky's like I originally planned."

"I'm glad you brought me here, Fabio," I said. "I stood in

the spot where the enchantress allegedly worked her voodoo and I felt nothing but peace and tranquility. I'm sorry you see it differently."

He didn't speak to me during the ride back into town. He deposited me in front of my house, which was more than I expected. The entire drive back I kept waiting for him to leave me on a deserted road so that I could walk my unclean feet home.

"Thank you for..." He was gone before I could finish the sentence.

"That went well, apparently," Gareth said from his position on the front porch.

I groaned. "You have no idea."

CHAPTER 16

I WENT into the library to return the Winnie the Pooh books I'd borrowed for Daniel. I'd wanted to introduce the angel to the sweet bear and his gang of friends, mostly so that Daniel knew he wasn't the only one who liked to wile away the hours thinking in a hundred acre wood.

The library was just as impressive as I remembered it. With its large atrium and multiple levels, it was like a mall for books. I still hadn't figured out the lay of the land, though, so I decided to seek out the librarian. I dropped off the books in the return section and noticed the librarian's office to the right.

Inside the small room, a woman sat behind a desk, thumbing through what appeared to be an old parchment. She looked middle-aged, her chestnut hair pulled into a severe bun. Her floral blouse was buttoned to the very top. The only thing missing was a thick pair of glasses.

She glanced up when I entered the room. "Welcome to the library," she said brightly. "How can I help you?"

"Hi, I'm looking for books about covens and I was hoping you could direct me to the right section."

The woman squinted at me. "Are you the new witch?"

"Yes, I'm Emma Hart."

It was only when she smiled that I realized the librarian was a vampire. I didn't know it was possible to be a vampire without sex appeal. Even Gareth, as annoying as he was, gave off a certain vibe. The librarian, however, appeared as uptight and pinched-faced as a harpy.

She stood to shake my hand. "Welcome to Spellbound. I'm Karen Duckworth. Town librarian."

"How long have you been the librarian here?" I asked. If she was a vampire, I wondered if she was one of the original members of the town.

"I took over when Harry retired," she said.

"Is Harry a vampire, too?"

Karen shook her head. "A wizard. He took me on as his apprentice several years before his retirement. He knew how much I loved information and he wanted the library in the right hands."

"Well, I'm here for information, so I hope you can help me."

Karen came out from behind the desk and walked with me to the atrium. "Information on witches and wizards can be found on the second floor. Would you like me to show you?"

"This place is so big, I wouldn't mind a little help. At least until I learn my way around."

Karen shuffled ahead of me and I noticed her calf-length pencil skirt paired with loafers. Two fashion styles that should never be on the same body at the same time. I was hardly a fashion guru, but even I knew that.

As we walked to the second floor, she nodded toward the sticker on my cardigan. "What is that?"

I glanced down, completely forgetting that this was the

cardigan I'd worn to speed dating. "Oh, it's from Thursday night speed dating."

She recoiled slightly. "Why would you do that?"

"If you need to ask, I guess you're not single."

Karen pressed her thin lips together. "I am, actually," she said. She didn't sound too happy about it.

"If you're not interested in speed dating, there's always a matchmaking service. I met with Pandora recently," I said. "She seems to have a lot of satisfied customers."

Karen paused in the stairwell and looked at me. "Didn't I hear that Demetrius Hunt was interested in you? You hardly seem like someone who needs the help of Pandora."

Silly me. I should've known better than to think that gossip didn't make it all the way to the library. I wasn't sure why I even cared about the librarian's relationship status. I'd been spending too much time thinking about Freddie, it seemed.

The second floor skirted the atrium and we walked halfway around the U-shape before reaching the section marked 'witches and wizards.' I immediately noticed a book entitled 'Covens and Cauldrons' and reached for it.

Karen laughed softly. "I can't tell you how odd it feels to have someone new to explain things to. You don't need to reach for the book. If you see a title you're interested in, just say it out loud and the book will come to you."

Talk about inspiring laziness. It was as bad as the Wish Market. Or as good, depending on your point of view.

"Covens and Cauldrons," I said. The heavy book shifted and slid off the shelf, floating into my hands. The cover was entirely black, with the only writing on the spine. "This looks old," I said. "There's no publication date." I thumbed through the pages. It wasn't like a typical book. There was no copy-right page, no table of contents, no dedication, and no index.

"It's been here a long time," Karen confirmed. "Have you received your grimoire yet? They're usually pretty old."

"My what?" I'd never heard of a grimoire. It sounded like a musical instrument.

"Your book of spells and charms," she explained. "All the witches in the coven have one. It's like the witches' manual."

"I guess I don't get a grimoire until I graduate from the academy," I said. "I'm still trying to master basic spells. I only earned my temporary broom license recently."

"Here's another book that might be useful to you," Karen said. "North American Covens." The book drifted from its place on the shelf and into Karen's hands. It was less dense than my book, probably because it only included covens on one continent.

"I don't know anything about my coven," I said. "It's possible the origin is European."

"It's a place to start," Karen said with a shrug. "If I were you, I'd start with the lighter text so you don't get over-whelmed."

Karen obviously didn't realize my background in law. Anyone who'd ever set foot in a law library could tell you how dense the books are. Statutes, regulations, amendments. The internet changed all that, of course. Not so in Spellbound.

"So are you the only librarian?" I asked.

"Yes, I'm the head librarian and I have two assistants. I do tend to be here the most, though. The library is my second home."

No wonder she didn't date much if she spent all her free time at the library.

"I've heard a lot of the vampires hang out at the Spell-bound Country Club. Do you ever golf? Or play tennis?"

Karen wrinkled her nose. "I'm not really into athletics or

sports. I prefer books. Unfortunately, I haven't met many vampires who feel the same way."

"You must've known Gareth," I said. "He's a huge fan of books."

"I always thought Gareth was gay," she said. "Imagine my surprise when he announced his engagement to Alison."

I burst out laughing. "You have to be the only person in Spellbound who figured that out."

"I think it's because I tend to observe more than interact. I notice things more than other residents." She hesitated. "You speak as though you know Gareth. I know you live in his house, but he died before you came, didn't he?"

"But that doesn't stop his ghost from haunting me," I said.

Her eyes widened. "You can see ghosts?"

"I can see his ghost, nobody else." Yet.

She tapped her finger against her cheek. "A witch who can see ghosts. How fascinating."

"And I also have an owl as my familiar. Apparently, that's not the done thing."

Karen laughed, and a few loose tendrils fell from her slick bun. "I'm a vampire librarian. I am all too familiar with that."

"I don't mean to overstep," I said, "but what's your relationship like with the other vampires? You're the first female I've met since I've been here. Where do the other girls hide?"

Karen leaned against one of the shelves. "To be honest, I don't really socialize much with anyone. I have my fur babies at home and my job here. My life is pretty full."

"But don't you miss companionship, having someone to talk to?" As much as Gareth could be a pain in my butt, I would miss him if he weren't around. Talking to Sedgwick wasn't the same.

"I tried dating a few decades ago," she said. "It didn't work out."

"Let me get this straight. You tried dating decades ago and

you've decided for the rest of your immortal life that you're done with it?"

She laughed. "Well, when you say it like that, it does sound rather ridiculous."

"Listen, there's speed dating every Thursday night at Cupid's Arrow. You should try it. My friends and I will go with you. If nothing else you'll meet some new friends to hang out with."

Karen frowned. "Is it just witches?"

"Absolutely not. It's everybody under the sun." Or not under the sun, as the case may be.

Karen seemed to consider it. "I'm free on Thursday evenings. Are you sure your friends won't mind?"

"Of course not. It'll be fun." And I had a feeling that Begonia would go nuts for the chance to make over Karen Duckworth. If anyone needed to vamp it up a little more, it was the vampire.

"So tell me the truth," Karen said. "Are you really going to speed dating to meet someone? I would think that if Demetrius Hunt wants to date you, then speed dating is more like low hanging fruit."

"Between you and me, I only went to look into Freddie's case. Apparently, he'd been a regular in the dating pool, so I wanted to speak with some of his former dates."

Karen's head drooped. "Poor Freddie. He's such a nice dwarf. He comes in now and then, usually looking for a new cookbook or something else to impress the ladies." She smiled, thinking about it. "The last time he was here…" She paused and her brow creased.

"What is it?"

Karen began walking briskly and I followed behind her. "I need to check something. He borrowed a book from a different section the last time he was here."

Was she really worrying about Freddie's overdue library book? That was the least of his concerns.

"I'm sure Freddie's sister can return the book for him," I said.

She jerked her head toward me, still walking. "It's not that. It's the type of book he checked out. I only just remembered this very moment. It wasn't his usual type." She arrived at a desk on the second floor and stood in front of a box of cards. "Freddie." A card lifted from the box.

"So what did he check out?"

"A spell book. Advanced Spells and Curses for the Overly Ambitious."

That didn't make any sense. Freddie was a dwarf. They tended not to use magic.

"Do you think Freddie knew that someone was going to curse him and he was trying to learn defensive spells?"

"I don't know," Karen said. "But I think it would be handy to find the book and see if he marked any pages in it."

"I'll go to his place right now," I said. "And I'd like to check out North American Covens, too."

"And I'll see you on Thursday night?" she asked, and I detected a note of eagerness in her voice.

"Meet us in the town square at eight o'clock."

I took my book and hurried from the library, anxious to get to Freddie's house. I had a strong feeling that the book was going to provide the answers that had been eluding us all.

I sent Sedgwick to Trixie's house with an urgent message. She arrived at Freddie's place more quickly than I expected, with her hair in curlers and slippers on her feet.

"I'd just gotten out of the shower," she said apologetically. "But the note sounded important."

"Did you bring the key?"

She held up the key to Freddie's door before unlocking it. "You think there's something there that will help?"

"Yes, I'm looking for a book called Advanced Spells and Curses for the Overly Ambitious."

The rooms were fairly cluttered, with books and newspapers piled high and knick-knacks aplenty. I laughed at a partially melted pot displayed on the mantel.

"Oh, you've spotted the crime against pottery," Trixie said with a wry smile.

"A childhood relic?" I queried.

"You would think," she said. "No, he and Heidi took a pottery class a couple of years ago. That was Freddie's attempt. He says Heidi insisted that he keep it, but I suspect he chose to keep it as a memento."

Like Lara and Thom. Now I was more certain than ever what I'd find here.

"Why is he using it to store paper?" I asked. I caught a glimpse of parchment sticking out of the top.

"Who knows with Freddie?" she said. "As you can see, he's not the tidiest dwarf on the planet."

"Where's his desk?" I asked.

"Other side of the kitchen."

I walked through the narrow kitchen to the desk. It was covered in papers but no sign of the library book.

"I'm going to try the bedroom," I said.

The thick book was plainly visible on the edge of the bedside table. A pink ribbon marked the page and I had every confidence that the ribbon had once adorned Heidi's hair.

Trixie padded into the room. "What did you find?"

"The truth," I said. As I skimmed the page, the realization washed over me. No one did this *to* him. Freddie did this to himself.

"Is it bad?" Trixie asked, her features etched with worry.

"Nothing that can't be undone. Not only do we have the Endless Sleep curse in here," I said, "but we also have the means to reverse it."

Trixie threw her arms around me and crushed me against her bosom. "Thank the sun and stars. Emma, I don't care what anyone says, you're the best."

"Um, thanks?" I tucked the book under my arm and slipped the pink ribbon into my pocket. I'd need both items to help Freddie, along with my wand.

Trixie's hand flew to her head. "I look a mess. I don't want Freddie to wake up and see me like this. He'll never let me live it down."

"If you hurry home now, you'll get there in time to welcome him back. I'll probably be a little slow anyway." Since I had no clue what I was doing.

Trixie scuttled outside and I quickly followed.

"Wait until Mother hears the news," she said. "She'll be thrilled."

"It might be a good time for a visit," I said. "You can deliver the news in person." We're only blessed with one mother, a fact I knew painfully well.

Trixie hugged me again. "You're right, Emma. You're absolutely right."

CHAPTER 17

I⟙ ⟙ⱺⱺĸ me seven attempts before I successfully reversed the spell. Thankfully, the only casualties were a few scorched pine trees and a hyperactive badger.

You're destroying my part of the forest, Sedgwick complained. *Now I'll never be able to hunt here.*

"Everything will grow back," I said. "And the badger will slow down...eventually." We watched as the small mammal performed somersaults across the forest floor.

Freddie finally stirred and my stomach clenched.

"Freddie?" I said softly.

His eyelids fluttered open. "Am I dead? Are you an angel?"

I turned to see the sunlight streaming through the trees behind me. It must have created a halo effect.

"No. My name is Emma. I'm the new witch in Spellbound. Welcome back, by the way."

He focused on my face. "You broke the spell?"

I reached inside the coffin and squeezed his hand. "Yes."

He lifted his round head and glared at me. "Why would you do that?"

I recoiled. "What do you mean? You've been in a glass casket in an endless sleep. Now you're awake." I was expecting a thank you, not dagger eyes.

"How long have I been asleep?" he asked.

"A couple of weeks."

"Weeks?" he spat. "Who gave you the right to wake me?"

Boy, was he angry. I didn't see that one coming.

"We thought you'd want to wake up. At first, we were trying to figure out who did this to you…"

Freddie pulled himself into a seated position and stretched his neck muscles. "No one did this to me. Didn't anyone see my letter?"

"What letter?"

He smacked his forehead. "Seriously? No one read my letter? I left it in the crime against pottery."

Oops. I guess that explained the piece of paper stuffed inside the pot. Seriously, though, who would think to look there?

"Why did you do this Freddie? People have been so upset. Your sister, your friends, especially Heidi."

His expression brightened at the mention of Heidi. "Has she been to see me?"

"Of course. She was a mess at your vigil."

This information seemed to please him. "How much of a mess? Like mascara dripping down her cheeks or just dabbing at her eyes with a tissue?"

"Um, somewhere in between?"

"Is she still with Paul?" I didn't miss the scowl that punctuated the satyr's name.

"I think so. At least she was the last time I saw her."

He slumped against the back of the coffin. "Then I'd like to go back to sleep. Can you trigger the curse again? You need the pink ribbon."

Trigger the curse? "Freddie, your family has been beside

themselves. Your niece and nephew miss their Uncle Freddie."

He stared into his lap. "I'd rather be asleep than live in this reality."

"Why?" I couldn't wrap my head around it. He'd rather be asleep, dreaming about who knows what...Oh. "Freddie, what did you dream about?"

He met my inquisitive gaze. "You've got me all figured out. What do you think? Her. It's always been her." He sighed. "At least in my dreams, we're together. We're in love and I've never been happier." His wistful tone made my heart ache.

"But the Heidi in your dream isn't the real Heidi," I said. "She's just a figment of your imagination."

"So what?" he countered. "It felt real. Isn't that what matters?"

Emotions stirred within me. As crazy as he sounded, his words resonated with me. If I could dream about a life with Daniel and it felt real, did it matter that it wasn't? For an insane moment, I considered building a coffin right next to Freddie's.

"You don't even know me," Freddie said. "Why do you care whether I was awake or asleep?"

"My friend Sophie was arrested for cursing you," I explained. "I knew she was innocent." And now I knew that *all* the suspects were innocent.

"Sophie Gale?" he queried, his brow creased with concern.

"Yes. She was the one who found you and then someone gave the sheriff false information." I waved a hand. "It was a mess, but it's done now."

"I didn't mean for anyone to take the blame," he said. "I left the letter and I made the coffin nice and comfortable. Why would someone do that if they wanted to curse me?"

My thoughts exactly.

"Can you do me a favor and help me out of here?" Freddie asked. "My legs are cramping up."

"Of course." I offered my arm and he used me to pull himself to a crouched position. Then he climbed over the edge of the coffin and dropped to the ground.

"Man, I didn't expect to be so stiff." He raised his arms over his head.

"You should probably see a healer," I said.

"Freddie?"

We both turned at the same time to see Heidi moving through the trees at a rapid pace.

"Heidi," he said, beaming.

He tried to move toward her, but his legs failed him and he stumbled. She reached him before he hit the ground and lifted him to his feet.

"Freddie, I can't believe it. You're awake." She kissed his cheek and wrapped her arms around him. "I've been so worried."

He closed his eyes, squeezing her tightly. "How did you know to come now?"

Heidi blushed. "I didn't. I come here every day to talk to you."

Freddie blinked. "Every day?"

"Of course. Why wouldn't I? I've missed you like crazy." She released him and stepped back to examine him. "The whole town has been looking into your curse."

I wasn't going to be the one to tell Heidi the truth. That had to come from Freddie.

Freddie took her by the hand. "I'm the one who did the curse, Heidi. I put myself in the coffin."

Heidi laughed. "Freddie, you shouldn't joke. Whoever did this to you needs to be locked up."

Freddie's expression remained serious. "I cursed myself, Heidi. I'm sorry. I didn't mean to hurt you."

"Why would you do such a thing?" she asked, going out of my mind."

"For you," he said softly. "I did it for you."

Her nose wrinkled. "I don't understand. How could cursing yourself be for my benefit?"

"Not for your benefit," he said, groping for words. "I just...I didn't want to live in a world where you and I weren't together."

"But we're together all the time," she chastised him.

"Not in the way I want," he said, avoiding her gaze.

"Freddie, look at me. Are you serious?"

"Would a joke about a thing like that?"

"I broke up with Paul yesterday," she said.

Freddie's head snapped to attention. "You what?"

"Ugh, I guess you finally found out he was cheating on you," I said. "Thank goodness. I hated knowing that."

Heidi looked at me blankly. "Paul was cheating on me?"

"Never mind," I said quickly and shuffled out of sight.

"I broke up with Paul because, while you were asleep, I realized that you were the one I truly wanted to be with." She placed her palms on his chubby cheeks. "You're the one I love, Freddie."

He pressed his lips to hers and I had to stop myself from cheering.

"True love's kiss would have broken the curse, too," I said. "If I'd screwed it up, I mean. There was a Plan B."

Heidi turned to look at me. "Thank you for bringing him back to me, Emma. I don't know how to live in a world without Freddie."

They kissed again.

I think that's your cue to leave, Sedgwick said from a nearby branch.

I found myself rooted to the ground, wishing for my own happily ever after.

Let's go, pervert.

I let out a deep sigh and followed my owl home.

CHAPTER 18

"ARE YOU SURE ABOUT THIS?" I asked. "It was my idea, so feel free to say no."

Daniel grinned at me. "Are you kidding? I'm so glad you came up with this." He wrapped his arm around me and squeezed. "I can always count on you to understand me."

The pixie at the reception desk fell over herself to greet us. I half expected a red carpet to unfurl beneath our feet.

"Welcome to Spellbound Care Home," she said. "Are you here to see a loved one?"

"We're here to see all the loved ones," Daniel replied. "Which way to the cafeteria? We're going to feed them with kindness and compassion."

The pixie seemed thrilled. "We're delighted to have volunteers. Go on through. Mrs. Murphy is waiting for you." I'd recently learned that Mrs. Murphy was in charge of facilities.

As we began to walk past the desk, she stopped me. "Ahem, your wand and broomstick, Miss Hart."

I held up my hands. "I didn't bring either today. You can frisk me if you like."

"No need." The pixie waved me through.

I showed Daniel the way to the cafeteria where Mrs. Murphy awaited our arrival.

"Good to see you, Mr. Starr," she said, pumping his hand. "It's not often we get people of your caliber in here. Usually, it's young ones for school credit, you see."

"This is my good friend, Emma Hart," he said.

Her smiled faded. "Yes, yes. I know the name. Made quite the mess in this place during her last visit."

"And I cleaned up after myself," I said defensively.

Mrs. Murphy softened. "That you did. Thank you." She bustled over to the kitchen area. "You'll both need to wear one of these." She held out two hairnets and I nearly laughed out loud. They were both covered in blue sparkles.

Daniel placed his over his blond hair without a word of protest and I immediately thought of Fabio, who refused to wear his helmet. Fabio was no Daniel—that much was certain.

"Here," he said. "Let me do yours." He took the blue hairnet and slid it over top of my head. "I think you need to pull up your hair first."

I bunched up my long hair and twisted it at the nape of my neck. He tucked the hair inside the net and admired his handiwork.

"You look so pretty. You should wear your hair up more often."

My mouth went dry and I turned away before I embarrassed myself.

"I especially like that birthmark at the nape of your neck. It looks like a little blue star."

I froze. A birthmark in the shape of a star? "I don't have a birthmark."

He touched the spot on my neck. "Right there. I guess you can't see it."

No, I couldn't, and yet Raisa knew it was there. I shivered. "Have you ever seen a birthmark like this one?"

"Can't say that I have, but I like it."

"Well, well," a familiar voice croaked. "Look what the owl dragged in."

"Hello Agnes," I said. "How are you?"

"Better now that you're here," she said. "Bring anything for me today?"

Not on your life. "I'm afraid not. I was under very strict orders."

A cackle escaped Agnes. "I'll bet. So how's that daughter of mine? Still got a wand stuck up her ass?"

"She says hello," I told her.

Agnes gave me an appraising look. "Does she really? Could've come to tell me herself."

"I'm working on it," I said. "For now, you'll need to be content with me serving you macaroni and cheese with breadcrumbs."

"No, I'll be content with *him* serving it." She held up her plate for Daniel. "I'd polish your halo anytime."

To his credit, Daniel wasn't the least bit fazed. He scooped a heaping spoonful of macaroni and cheese onto her plate.

"Where's your boyfriend?" I asked.

"He's *not* my boyfriend," Agnes objected, and I realized how much fun it was to get a rise out of her.

"I'm right here," Silas said, drifting to the counter. "I heard we had special guests today. Very exciting."

Estella floated in behind him. "I'm so glad you're here so I can thank you in person. I have my Freddie back and Trixie has come to see me. She's even set up a regular visitation schedule."

"That's great news," I told her.

"When you're finished your macaroni," I said to Agnes, "can we talk about those six cards you dealt me last time?"

Agnes launched an eyebrow. "Only if you brought the necessary lubricant."

At the mention of lubricant, Silas drifted closer to her. "What's this?"

She elbowed him in the ribs. "For my lips," she snapped.

He flashed a wicked grin. "Even better."

Daniel laughed. "Is it always like this here?"

"Pretty much," I replied.

"Excellent," he said. "Let's put it on the calendar again for next week. I want it to be part of my regular schedule."

I rolled my eyes skyward, fairly certain that no one was listening.

Somebody save me.

Daniel handed me the slotted spoon. "Your turn." His fingers brushed against mine and my heart filled with joy.

Then again, maybe somebody already had.

* * *

Sign up for my newsletter via my website at www.annabelchase.com and like me on <u>Facebook</u> so you can find out about new releases and sales.

Grab the next book in the series—

Lucky Charm, Book 4

More Series by Annabel Chase

Starry Hollow Witches

Federal Bureau of Magic

Divine Place

Hex Support Mystery

Spellslingers Academy of Magic

Demonspawn Academy

Magic Bullet

Pandora's Pride

Midnight Empire

Made in the USA
Las Vegas, NV
16 April 2023